**Ryan didn't have a huge number of pictures, but there were a few Beth remembered, including one of a wild, rugged landscape that had hung over his bed, and it made her body tingle to look at it.**

How many times had they made love on the bed beneath it? Dozens, every one of them memorable. She put it to one side and sorted through the others, the less contentious ones. Or less evocative, at least, of their past, the pre-Grace period before he'd gone away for the first time, when their lovemaking was smoking hot and nothing else was taken seriously.

He'd made her laugh, made her gasp with ecstasy and weep with frustration, but always, always, he'd set her on fire. It had been the perfect antidote to Rick's cheating and lying ways, and just what she'd needed. Intensely passionate, and yet light and frivolous—or it would have been if things hadn't turned out the way they had, but the heat, the passion, was still there smoldering under the surface, and it was getting harder to ignore.

Dear Reader,

Well, this is book 101. Easy, you'd think, after all that practice? Apparently not, because there are only so many ways you can skin a rabbit, and I'm struggling to find issues that I haven't already covered, often more than once. I know every story is different, but even so…

So I decided to tackle an issue I've largely avoided over the years, because it's such a sensitive and emotive subject. It's also, though, a very real issue, and one which affects a surprising number of couples—the loss of a stillborn child. It was hard to write, and I sincerely hope I've done it justice.

Ryan and Beth hardly knew each other when she became pregnant, and the loss of their baby wounded them both deeply, but their grief isolated them from each other. Now back working in the ED after two years apart, their attraction still strong, they need to find a way forward. Enter Tatty, a scruffy stray dog who steals Ryan's heart and helps them find the way. She may have stolen the show a teensy bit, but I hope you fall under her spell the way Beth and Ryan did.

With love,

*Caroline* x

# FROM HEARTACHE
# TO FOREVER

———

## CAROLINE ANDERSON

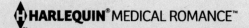
HARLEQUIN® MEDICAL ROMANCE™

Recycling programs
for this product may
not exist in your area.

ISBN-13: 978-1-335-64183-0

From Heartache to Forever

First North American Publication 2019

Copyright © 2019 by Caroline Anderson

This edition published by arrangement with Harlequin Books S.A.

For questions and comments about the quality of this book, please contact us at CustomerService@Harlequin.com.

Printed in U.S.A.

**Books by Caroline Anderson**

**Harlequin Medical Romance**

*Hope Children's Hospital*

*One Night, One Unexpected Miracle*

*Yoxburgh Park Hospital*

*From Christmas to Eternity*
*The Secret in His Heart*
*Risk of a Lifetime*
*Their Meant-to-Be Baby*
*The Midwife's Longed-For Baby*
*Bound by Their Babies*
*Their Own Little Miracle*
*A Single Dad to Heal Her Heart*

**Harlequin Romance**

*The Valtieri Baby*
*Snowed in with the Billionaire*
*Best Friend to Wife and Mother?*

Visit the Author Profile page
at Harlequin.com for more titles.

# CHAPTER ONE

'Ah, Beth, just the person. I've got a favour to ask you.'

Her heart sank. *Again?*

'How did I know that was coming, right at the end of my shift?'

She turned towards James with a wry smile and then everything ground to a halt, because the man standing beside the ED's clinical lead was painfully, gut-wrenchingly familiar.

His strangely piercing ice blue eyes locked on hers, his mouth opening as if to speak, but James was still talking, oblivious to the tension running between them.

'Beth, this is Ryan McKenna, our new locum consultant. Ryan, this is—'

'Hello, Beth.'

Her name was a gentle murmur, his eyes softening as he took a step forward and

gathered her up against his chest in a hug
so warm, so welcome that it brought tears
to her eyes.

'Oh, Ry—'

He let her go long before she was ready,
stared down into her eyes and feathered a
kiss on her cheek.

'OK. So I'm guessing you two know each
other already, or this is love at first sight,'
James said drily, and Ryan laughed a little off
kilter, taking a step back and giving her some
much-needed space to drag herself together.

'Yeah, we know each other,' Ryan said,
his voice oddly gruff. 'We—er—we worked
together, before I went abroad. Best scrub
nurse I've ever had the privilege of working with.'

There was a whole world left unsaid, but
James just nodded, still unaware of the turmoil going on under his nose.

'Well, it's good to know you got on—we
rely on teamwork. Beth, I was going to ask
you if you could be a star and give Ryan the
once-over of the department and then take
him for a coffee? They really need me in
Resus, and I'm sure you'd like to catch up?'

'What, now?' she asked, feeling a flicker
of something that could have been panic.

'If you can spare the time. I'd be really grateful and they do need me.'

She met Ryan's eyes, one eyebrow raised a fraction. 'Are you OK with this?' he murmured.

As if James had left her with a choice…

'It's fine, Ry. I don't have to be anywhere,' she said quietly, surrendering to the inevitable, and she turned back to James. 'Go. You're right, they could really use you. Sam's tearing his hair out and Livvy's rushed off her feet. We'll be fine.'

He nodded, his face relieved. 'Thanks, Beth. You're a star. And while you're at it, if you could convince him to apply for the permanent post, you'll have my undying gratitude.'

Her heart thudded, the flicker threatening to turn into a full-on panic attack.

'I thought the application window was closed?'

'It's been extended. So—if you could twist his arm?'

He was smiling, but his meaning was clear, and they were desperate for another consultant, but simply seeing Ryan again had sent her emotions into freefall and her hard-won status quo felt suddenly threatened. A locum post was one thing, but she didn't know if she could cope with him here on a permanent basis, not when she was finally putting her life and her heart back together after the last two agonising years.

Not that it, or she, would ever be the same again...

Anyway, it wasn't relevant, because he was committed to Medicine For All, the aid organisation he'd been working with for the past two years, and she knew how strongly he felt about that. He'd walked away from Katie because she didn't understand, so there was no way he'd be looking for a permanent job and he obviously hadn't been clear enough with James.

'Leave it with me,' she said, which wasn't a yes but it was the best she could do, because she was oddly torn between wanting to run away and wanting to talk to him, to find out how he was.

Because something had changed him, she could see that at a glance. He was thinner, his face slightly drawn, shadows lurking in the back of his eyes. The same shadows that lurked in hers after all that had happened between them? Or other shadows, from the things he'd seen in those two years? Both, probably.

'Sure?' James asked, maybe finally picking up on the tension running between them, and she nodded.

'I'm sure. Go. Leave it to me.'

'Thank you. I know you'll do your best. I'll see you on Monday, Ryan. I'm really pleased you've agreed to join us.'

'So am I. I'll look forward to working with you.'

They shook hands and she watched James go, then Ryan turned back to her with a wry smile that touched her heart.

'Forget the guided tour. Is there somewhere quiet we can go and get a coffee?'

She felt a wave of relief and nodded. 'Yes. There's a café that opens onto the park. We can sit outside.'

The café was busy, but they found a little bistro table bathed in April sunshine and tucked out of the way so they could talk without being overheard, and he settled opposite her and met her eyes, his searching.

'So, how are you?'

Her heart thumped. 'Oh—you know.' She tried to smile. 'Getting there, bit by bit. You?'

That wry, sad smile again, flickering for an instant and then gone. 'I'm OK.'

She wasn't sure she believed him, but there was something else...

'So, how come you're here, in Yoxburgh? Is that deliberate?' she asked, needing to know if he'd sought her out or just stumbled on her by accident, but he nodded slowly.

'Yoxburgh? Yes, sort of. I needed a job, there was one here, and I know it's a lovely place. But I didn't know you were here, if that's what you're asking, not until I saw you.'

'Would you have applied if you'd known?'

He shrugged. 'Not without talking to you first to see if you were OK with it.'

'Why? If you needed a job—'

'There are plenty of jobs.'

'But not here.'

'No. Not here, and I wanted to be here, but now—well, that depends.'

Her heart hiccupped. 'On?'

'You, of course. If you're working in the ED, we'll probably be working together. I'm OK with that, we worked well together before, but us—you and me—that's different. Much more complicated, and the last thing I want is to make things difficult for you, so I need to know if you're going to be OK with me being underfoot all the time.'

Was she?

'Just so long as you don't expect to pick up where we left off. Well, not that, obviously, but—you know. Before...'

He frowned, his eyes raw. 'I don't expect anything, Beth. The way we left things, I've got no right to expect anything. For all I know you might be back with Rick.'

'Rick?' It startled a laugh out of her because after everything that had happened Rick was so far off her radar it was almost funny. 'No way. He was a lying cheat, why would I be back with him, any more than you'd be back with Katie?'

He gave a startled laugh. 'OK, I can see that, but—someone?'

'No. It's just me, and I'm happy that way. You?'

He laughed again. 'Me? I haven't had time to breathe, never mind get involved with anyone. Anyway, people get expectations and then it all gets messy.'

'Not everyone's like Katie.'

'No. They're not.' He studied her, his eyes stroking tenderly over her face. She could almost feel their touch, but then he closed them and shook his head with a little laugh. 'I can't believe you're in the ED. What brought that on? I thought Theatre was your life.'

'You can talk. I thought surgery was *your* life.'

He shrugged. 'People change. I was facing a lifetime of increasing specialisation, and I didn't want to spend every day doing the same thing over and over again until I'd perfected it. I wanted a change, and MFA provided me with that, and over the course of my time with them I realised I like trauma work. I like the variety, the pace, but you...'

'I wanted a change, too.' Needed a change, because everywhere she'd looked there'd been reminders of what she'd lost, and she'd found working in Theatre with anyone but him just plain wrong. 'So, when did you get back?'

'Two weeks ago. I've been back a few times on leave, picked up a bit of locum work here and there to refill the coffers and keep my registration up to date, but this time it's for good.'

*For good?*

She felt her eyes widen, and her heart thumped. 'Really?'

His smile was sad. 'Yes, really. I've seen enough horror, lost some good friends, seen way too many dead chil—'

She flinched, and he gave a quiet groan. 'Sorry. I didn't...'

'It's OK,' she lied. 'And I can only begin to imagine what it must have been like. So, was it after you lost your friends you decided to come back?'

He gave a wry laugh. 'No. Oddly, that was when I decided to stay on longer, to carry on the work they were doing because it was so necessary, but there'll always be others waiting to take my place and it was time to come home because I'm just as needed here in many ways. My grandparents are frail and my mother's shouldering the whole burden on her own, and it just seemed like it was time. Time to move on with my life, to get back to the day job, as it were. Back to the future.'

With her?

He'd said it was time to move on with his life, but he was the one who didn't do relationships. Not after Katie had tried to get pregnant to stop him going away.

But what if he'd changed now, got MFA

out of his system and was ready to settle down? It sounded like it, and maybe he wanted to try again with her? Maybe a bit more seriously this time—although it could hardly have been more serious than the way it had turned out. But if he did?

She wasn't sure she was ready for that, not yet. She was still working through life day by day, hour by hour, step by step. She stared down into her coffee, stirring the froth mindlessly.

'So that's me,' he murmured. 'How about you? Are you happy here, in Yoxburgh?'

Happy? She could hardly remember what that felt like.

'As happy as I can be anywhere,' she said honestly. 'It's a lovely place, and that weekend we spent here—it was really special, the walks, the feel of the sea air—we said then what an amazing place it would be to live, and then a job came up here and I thought, why not? I was sick of working in an inner city, the noise and the dirt and the chaos, and I wanted to get away from all the reminders. I just needed peace.'

Peace to heal, to reconcile herself, to learn to live again, and where better than here, where it all began—

She sucked in a breath and looked up again. 'So how come you applied for the locum job?'

He shrugged. 'Same reason, I guess. I loved it here, the peace, the tranquillity of the coast and the countryside, and I needed that, after all I've seen. And there were the memories. I know we were only here for a weekend, but it was hugely significant.'

He looked away, his brow creased in a thoughtful frown, then he looked back and met her eyes. 'If I'd known you were pregnant, Beth, I wouldn't have gone away—not then, at least. I would have found a way out of it, delayed it or something. Not that it would have changed anything, but at least I could have been there for you. And I did try when I knew, but you didn't seem to want me there, and I couldn't really do anything anyway, nothing constructive, so I left and I tried to airbrush you out of my life, out of my thoughts, but I couldn't. I realised that, the moment I got back when all I could think about was seeing you again, making sure you were all right.'

He'd tried to airbrush her out of his thoughts? And failed? Well, that made two of them. Even so...

'Why didn't you act on it? You've been back two weeks and you haven't contacted me.'

'You've changed your phone number.'

She felt a twinge of guilt. 'I know. I'm sorry, I suppose I should have told you. But you could have found me if you'd really wanted to. You know enough people.'

He nodded. 'You're right, and I was going to as soon as I knew what I was doing, where I was going to be, but whatever, I've found you now, I'm here, I'm back for good, and at least I know you're all right. Well, as all right as you can be, I guess.'

Their eyes locked, his heavy with understanding, and she felt her heart quiver.

'I've missed you,' she said, the admission wrung from her without her consent, and he smiled sadly.

'I've missed you, too. I didn't realise how much, until I saw you again. All that airbrushing just didn't work.'

Her eyes welled, and she blinked the tears away.

'Ry, I'm not the person I was. I've changed.'

'I'm sure you have. So have I. Don't worry, I don't expect anything, Beth, but it is good to see you again and I'm so sorry I let you down. I wish I could undo it.'

She nodded, looking away from those all-seeing eyes, turning her attention back to the froth on her coffee. She poked the last bit of froth with the spoon, then looked up again.

'So if you really are done with MFA, are you going for the permanent post? James was groaning the other day about the calibre of the applicants so they've obviously had to extend the closing date, and it sounds like he wants you to apply.'

He looked thoughtful. 'That depends.'

'On?'

'You, again, of course.' He shrugged again. 'I don't want to do something that you don't want, Beth. If you don't want me here, I won't apply, especially since we'll be working together. I know I've accepted the locum job, but if that's an issue, too, I can always pull out. I haven't signed anything yet.'

She frowned at him. 'But you've said you'll do it! You'd never go back on your word.'

'I would if it would hurt you. The last thing I want is to hurt you again.'

She shook her head. 'You didn't hurt me, not like Rick hurt me. You didn't lie and cheat and sleep with my best friend and then pretend it was over when it wasn't. Your only failing was your commitment to Medicine For All, but I got that. I understood, and I admired you for it.'

'Katie didn't.'

'I know, but I'm not Katie, and you're not Rick, and you've never hurt me. And you were there for me when it mattered, and you stayed until it was over. That meant so much.'

'I could have stayed longer. *Should* have stayed longer.'

'No. I didn't want you to, Ryan. You needed to go back, to fulfil your commitments, and I needed to be on my own. You were right, you couldn't do anything constructive to help me, and there were people in other parts of the world who really did need you. Don't feel guilty.'

'But I do.'

'Well, don't. I don't need your guilt, I've got enough burdens. You did the right thing.'

She straightened up and smiled at him, pushing back the shadows. 'Why don't I give you that guided tour James was talking about, and introduce you to some of the others? And then you can decide if you want to apply.'

'You don't mind? I might get it. You have to be sure.'

She shrugged. 'Ryan, we're in desperate need of another consultant and I can't stand in the way of that, but I can't promise you a future with me, not in any way, so if you're thinking of applying because of that—'

'I'm not. I've told you, I don't expect anything from you.'

'Good. Let's go and do this, then.'

The department was much as expected— modern, well equipped, but ridiculously busy, and he could see why he was needed.

And they had a permanent post going. It would be a great job, a perfect place to settle down—with Beth?

No. She'd warned him off, said she'd changed, and so had he, and yet he'd still felt his heart slam against his chest at the sight of her, felt a surge of something utterly unexpected when he'd pulled her into his arms and hugged her.

*Love?*

Of course not. He didn't do love, not any more, and anyway, it wouldn't work. She wanted other things from life, things he didn't want, things that didn't include him, but they could still be friends. They could work on that, and it was still a great hospital in a beautiful part of England. What more could a man want? And anyway, it was only a temporary post at the moment. It wasn't like he was committed. If they couldn't work together, he could always leave it at that and move on.

'Seen enough?'

He met her soft grey-green eyes, so bad at hiding her feelings, and he could tell she wanted to get away.

'Yes. Thank you, Beth. I need to get on, anyway, I've got to find somewhere to live by Monday. Any idea who to ask?'

'Hang on, Livvy Henderson might know.' She stuck her head back into Resus. 'Livvy, do you know if anyone's moved into the house you were renting? Ryan's looking for somewhere.'

'Ah, no, Ben's got a new tenant.' She flashed him a smile. 'Sorry I can't help. I hope you find something, Ryan.'

'I'm sure I will. Never mind. Thanks.' He turned back to Beth. 'So—any other ideas?'

'Baldwins? They've got a few properties near me advertised to let. Might be worth asking them. They've got an office on the High Street. It depends what you want.'

He laughed, thinking of some of the places he'd slept in over the past two years, and shook his head. 'I'm not fussy. Just so long as it has a garden. I need to be able to get outside. And somewhere to park would be handy.'

'Go and see them. I'm sure they'll have something.'

He nodded. 'I will. Thank you. I was thinking I'd check into a hotel and maybe look at some places tomorrow.'

Something flickered in her eyes and then was gone, as if she'd changed her mind. 'Good idea,' she said, but nothing more, and he wondered what she'd been going to say. Whatever, she'd thought better of it, and he realised he had some serious work to do to rebuild their friendship.

Baby steps, he thought, and then felt a stab of pain.

'Right. Well, I'll see you on Monday.'

The eyes flickered again, and he could see the moment she changed her mind. 'Give me a call, tell me how you get on.'

'I don't have your number, remember.' And nobody changed their number unless they wanted to hide, so from whom? Rick? Him? Or from the others, the well-meaning friends who hadn't quite known what to say to her? He could understand that. He'd blocked quite a few numbers.

He pulled out his phone and found her entry. 'OK, give it to me?' Then he rang her, and heard her phone buzz in her pocket.

'OK. I'll let you know how I get on with— Baldwins?'

'Yup. Good luck.'

Was it those words, or was it just that the fates had finished playing Russian roulette with him?

Whatever, the agent showed him a whole bunch of stuff, none of which appealed, and then said, very carefully, 'There is something else. It was for sale but it didn't shift, so the owner got tenants in and they've done a runner and left it in a state, but he's disabled and can't afford to pay someone to sort it out, so if you didn't mind rolling up your sleeves I'm sure I could negotiate a discount. It's a great place, or it could be. It's a three-bed bungalow on Ferry Lane, overlooking the marshes and the harbour, and you can see the boats on the river in the distance.'

The river? He could feel his pulse pick up. 'Does it have a drive?'

'Oh, yes, and a double garage and a big garden. They had a dog so the house smells a bit, but with a good clean and a tidy-up...'

'Can I see it?' he asked, impatient now, because it sounded perfect, doggy or not, and he'd grown up with dogs.

The agent glanced at his watch. 'I can't take you today, I'm on my own here, and I'm out of the office until eleven tomorrow, but I can give you the key. I take it you're trustworthy?'

Ryan laughed. 'I think so. After all, what can I do to it that the tenants haven't? Apart from clean it?'

'Good point. Here. And take my card and give me a call.'

'I will. Thanks.'

He hefted the key in his hand, slid it into his pocket and headed back to the car, cruising slowly along the clifftop before turning onto Ferry Lane and checking out the numbers. And there it was, a tired-looking bungalow set back at the top of a long concrete drive with weeds growing in the cracks.

Uninspiring, to say the least, and it didn't get better as he went up the drive, but as he got out of the car he caught sight of the view and felt peace steal over him.

He slid the key into the lock, went through the front door and was confronted by multi-coloured chaos.

The agent was right, it did smell of dog, the kitchen and bathroom were filthy, and the garden was a jungle, but every time he looked out of a window and saw the river in the distance his heart beat a little faster.

It might be awful now, but with a good scrub, the carpets cleaned and the grass cut, it would be transformed. Oh, and about a vat and a half of white paint to cover the lurid walls and calm it all down. All he had to do was roll up his sleeves and get stuck in.

He pulled out his phone and rang the agent.

'I'll take it,' he said, and the man laughed.

'I thought you might. Your eyes lit up when I mentioned the river.'

'Yup.' He laughed. 'So, where do we go from here? It's just that I am in quite a hurry, I start work on Monday. Is there any danger we can sort it by then?'

'Yes, we can do it today. We're open until seven tonight. If you come in at six, that'll give me time to get it all sorted.'

So he rang Beth, although he hadn't meant to, and told her about it.

'Where is it?'

'Just up Ferry Lane on the left. It's number eleven.'

'Are you still there?'

'Yes—why?'

'Can I come? I'm only round the corner and I have to see this.'

He laughed. 'Sure. You'll be shocked, it's pretty dire, but I'll get my body weight in cleaning materials and paint and it'll be fine.'

'It can't be that bad.'

He just laughed again, and went outside to wait for her.


'Oh, my word...'

'Yeah. Great, isn't it? You've got to love the shocking pink. But look.'

He wrapped her shoulders in his warm, firm hands and turned her gently towards the window, and she felt her breath catch. 'Oh—you can see the river! It's where we walked that day—'

The day he'd lifted her off the stile and into his arms and kissed her, and she'd fallen a little bit in love with him. The day it had all begun...

'I know,' he murmured, his voice a little gruff. 'It's beautiful down there, and the thought of having it on my doorstep, being able to look at it all the time, is just amazing.' He dropped his hands and stepped away from her, but she could still feel the echo of his fingers, the warmth that had radiated off his body.

'Come and see the rest. He said it's got three bedrooms but I only got as far as the first one and gave up.'

She could see why. The place was dirty and untidy, as if the tenants had picked up their things and walked away without a backward glance, and there was a pervading odour of dog. There was a lot to do before it was a home.

They walked through it, examining all the rooms, finding the third bedroom at the opposite end to the other two, tucked away beyond the kitchen with a patio door to the garden. It even had an en suite shower room.

'So will you make this your bedroom?'

He shook his head. 'No. I'll use it as a study because of the door to the garden. Do you know what, the house is actually in pretty good condition under all the dirt. I don't think it'll take a lot to turn it around.'

She eyed the grubby carpets, the faded curtains, the filthy bathroom. 'If you say so.'

'It's only dirt. I'll get on it in the morning. I've got to go down to the office now to sign something, then I need to eat and find a bed for the night. Any suggestions?'

Why? Why did she say it? She had no idea, but without her consent her mouth opened.

'I've got a spare room, and a casserole in the slow cooker that's enough for three meals so that should do us, so we can eat after you've done the paperwork and then come back here and make a start if you like? I'm on early tomorrow but I can help you now, and again after my shift. Bear in mind it's Friday tomorrow, so you've only got three days before you start work and I guess you've got other stuff to do first. Like find some furniture, for starters.'

He laughed. 'Furniture would be handy.' His smile faded as he searched her eyes, his own unreadable. 'Beth, are you sure? That's a lot to ask.'

Sure? She wasn't in the slightest bit sure, but it seemed the sensible thing to do, the most practical, and she was nothing if not practical.

'I'm sure,' she lied. 'And anyway, you didn't ask, I offered.'

She just hoped it wasn't a huge mistake.


It was just as well she'd agreed to help, because the house was worse than he'd thought.

After they'd eaten he changed into jeans, rolled up his sleeves and they went straight back to tackle the mess, armed with the contents of her cleaning cupboard. She hit the kitchen while he tore up the bedroom carpets, and by the time he'd done that it looked a whole lot better. Then he studied the sitting room carpet.

Was it salvageable? Doubtful, but with a clean...

He turned back the corner to see what was underneath, and blinked. Seriously? An original wood block floor? He pulled back more, then more, and started to laugh because it was so unexpected and wonderful.

'Hey, come and see this,' he called, and Beth went into the sitting room, clad in shocking pink rubber gloves that matched the awful walls, a streak of dirt on her cheek, and his heart crashed against his ribs.

*How could she look so sexy?*

'Wow! That's amazing. It's gorgeous!'

It wasn't alone. He dragged his eyes off her, looking way more appealing than she had any right to look with dirt on her face and her hair all sweaty, and studied the floor. 'Well, I don't know about gorgeous, but it knocks spots off the carpet and it'll save me money. I wonder if the hall's the same?'

It was, so was the dining room, and he was stunned.

'It's incredible. I love it. I think you're right, a bit of polish and it will be gorgeous. Right, let's go. It's late, you're working tomorrow and I could kill for a cup of tea.'

'Me, too. It might wash the dust out of my throat.'

He chuckled, and her eyes softened with her smile. Without thinking, he pulled her into his arms and hugged her, burying his face in her hair and breathing in dust and bleach and something else, something familiar that made his heart ache.

'Thank you. Thank you so much for all you've done. You've been amazing and I wouldn't have got nearly as far without you.'

She eased away, leaving him feeling a little awkward and a bit bereft. 'Yeah, you would, because you wouldn't have stopped. Right, time to go.'

* * *

'Tea or coffee?'

'Tea would be lovely, thank you. Want a hand?'

'No, you're fine. Go and relax, I won't be long.'

Relax? He was too wired for that, and stiffening up nicely after all the heaving and bending. He was going to hurt in the morning. Ah, well. At least they'd made a start.

He flexed his shoulders and strolled over to the shelves in the corner of her sitting room beside the fireplace, where a silver trinket box had caught his eye. It was a heart, he discovered, smooth and rounded, incredibly simple but somehow beautiful, and crying out to be touched.

He picked it up, and it settled neatly into the palm of his hand as if it belonged there, the metal cool against his palm, the surface so smooth it felt like silk. There was something written on it, he realised, and he traced it with his fingertip, his heart starting to pound as he read the tiny inscription.

A date. A date he recognised, a date he could never forget because it was carved on his heart, too.

He heard her footsteps behind him.

'Tea,' she said, her voice sounding far away, the clink of the mugs as she put them down oddly loud in the silence. He turned slowly towards her, the heart still nestled in the palm of his hand.

'What's this?' he asked gruffly, knowing the answer, and her smile nearly broke his heart.

'Her ashes.'

Her face blurred, and he bent his head and lifted the tiny urn to his lips, his eyes squeezed tightly shut to trap the tears inside.

'You kept them,' he said, when he could speak.

'Of course. I didn't know what else to do. You weren't there by the time I picked them up, and I didn't want to stay where we were because of all the reminders and I knew if they were there I'd feel tied, so I had to keep her with me until we could decide together what to do.'

He looked up, blinking so he could see her face, and her smile cracked.

'Oh, Beth...'

He reached out his free arm and pulled her against his side, and she laid her hand over the delicate little urn in his hand, her fingers curling round over his as she rested her head on his shoulder.

'Grace didn't suffer, Ry. At least we know that.'

He nodded, and she lifted the little heart gently out of his hand, kissed it and put it back on the shelf, next to a pretty cardboard box. She touched it fleetingly.

'That's her memory box,' she said softly. 'The midwives gave it to me in the hospital. Would you like to see it?'

He shook his head, mentally backing away from it, unable to face it. 'No. Not tonight. I'm too tired, Beth. I think I might head up to bed. I've got another long day tomorrow and you're working.'

Her smile was understanding, as if she'd seen straight through him.

'When you're ready,' she said gently, but he'd spent two long years running away from it and he wasn't sure he'd ever be ready for what he knew must be in that memory box.

Time to stop running? Maybe, but not now. Not tonight.

Not yet…

# CHAPTER TWO

'ARE YOU OK?'

Ryan propped himself against the doorframe of his newly acquired home and gave her a slightly crooked smile.

'Yeah, I'm fine.'

'Are you sure? Because you didn't look it last night.'

He hadn't felt it, and between the memories that the little heart had dragged up out of their hiding place and the knowledge that Beth was just on the other side of the wall, he'd hardly slept at all. And then seeing this place in daylight, realising the enormity of the task, had made him wonder what on earth he was doing.

So, yeah, one way and another, he was very far from fine.

He scrubbed a hand through his hair and shrugged away from the doorframe, stepping back into the hall to let her in. 'I was tired. And, yes, OK, I was—uh—I was a bit emotional. It was just holding it, you know? Knowing Grace was in there.'

She nodded. 'I know.' Her smile faltered, and she sucked in a breath and looked around, then blinked. 'Oh—wow! What happened to the pink?'

He laughed. 'Three coats of white paint happened to it.'

'Three? Already? What are you, Superman?'

'It's been a nice breezy day and I've had all the windows open so the paint's dried quickly and it really doesn't take that long. I've done the sitting room, as well. Have a look.'

He pushed the door open and followed her in, and she gasped.

'Oh! It looks so much bigger. And brighter.'

He chuckled. 'That wouldn't be hard. Cup of tea?'

'That would be lovely. I haven't had a lot to drink today. I've brought scruffy clothes.'

He frowned at her. 'You've been working all day.'

'So? It was the sensible Friday shift. The late shift won't have it so easy.'

He headed for the kitchen. 'Tea or coffee? I bought a kettle and some mugs and stuff.'

'Tea, please.'

He felt her watching him dunking tea bags, pouring milk, his hands covered in paint. There was some in his hair, too, he'd noticed. He was going to have to do some serious scrubbing to get it off by Monday.

'So how was work?' he asked, handing her the mug. 'Anything interesting?'

'Not really, a few sporting and gardening injuries, the odd fall, but nothing nasty, just busy.'

He thought of his average day with MFA and laughed. 'I'll take that.'

'I guessed you would. Bit of a change from what you've been doing.'

'Yeah.' He put away the memories and conjured up a smile. 'Here—let's go in the garden. I found a bench. It's a bit wobbly, but it should be OK if we sit down carefully.'

He scooped up a packet of biscuits and she followed him through the dining room and the tired conservatory into the garden.

She eyed the bench dubiously as it creaked under his weight. 'I think I'll sit here,' she said, taking a biscuit and perching on the edge of the steps that led up to the garden from the patio. Well, patio was a bit of a stretch. Some uneven crazy paving, but it was somewhere to put a table and chairs.

'It's a pretty garden.'

He snorted, but she stuck to her guns. 'It is! Look at the perennials in the border.'

'I see them. I also see the weeds, and the foot-high grass, and the fence that's making a bid for freedom. I don't think this place has had any maintenance in living memory but hey, it'll give me something to do in my time off. That'll be a bit of a luxury.'

'Time off?'

He nodded. 'Yeah, you don't get a lot of that in the field. You only do three months at a time, but it's pretty full on.' He fell silent, his thoughts obviously miles away, and she wondered what he was seeing. Probably just as well not to know.

'Here, have another biscuit before I eat them all.'

He got up to hand her the packet, and as he pushed himself up the bench creaked again and slid over sideways into a heap.

She laughed. She tried not to, but his face was a picture and she dissolved into giggles.

'How is that funny?' he asked, but his lips

were twitching and seconds later he was sitting beside her on the steps, clutching his stomach and laughing just as helplessly as her.

'Maybe you need to invest in some new garden furniture,' she suggested when she could speak again, and he nodded.

'Maybe. Or I can sit here and study the windows. They really need replacing.'

'Buy a new bench. It's cheaper than the windows and you don't own the house.'

'No, I don't. Not yet.'

Yet? She turned and met his eyes.

'Yet?'

'It's possibly for sale.'

'But—you're a locum! Why would you buy it?'

'Well, I wouldn't, unless I was going to be living here long term.' He paused, looked away, then looked back, his eyes searching hers. 'I think I want to apply for the permanent job.'

She wasn't expecting that, not so soon, not before he'd even started work there, but realistically what was there to know? He'd met James and a few of the others, he knew her, he knew he loved the town—what more was there?

Nothing—except her, and her feelings, and if he'd asked her what they were she'd be hard pushed to tell him, because after seeing him with Grace's heart last night they were even more confused. She looked away.

'I'd give it a few days before you decide. You might hate it.'

'Unlikely, and I can always withdraw my application if I want to.'

'Withdraw it?' She laughed. 'You seriously think James wouldn't talk you out of doing that?'

'I know he wouldn't. Not if I don't want to be talked out of it. If you don't want me here, Beth, I'll go, no matter how much James wants me to stay.'

She searched his eyes, read the sincerity in them, the concern for her welfare. And then she thought of the little silver heart that had fitted so perfectly in the palm of his hand...

She wanted him to stay.

It was the last thing she'd expected to feel and she had no idea where it had come from, but it hit like a lightning bolt, and she sucked in a breath and got to her feet.

'Let's just see,' she said, tipping out the dregs of her tea onto the weedy grass behind her. 'So—what's next?'

'My bedroom. I'm picking up my clothes and other stuff from my mother's on Sunday, and I can borrow her airbed.'

'Airbed?' She turned and stared at him. 'Ry, there's no hurry. You can stay with me as long as you want.'

He shook his head. 'No. I've put you out quite enough, Beth. I'll stay tonight and to-morrow, but then I'll be here.'

'But—you've got no furniture. It's a bit basic,' she murmured, but he just laughed.

'Basic? Having a roof is a luxury in some of the places I've been. Trust me, this is a palace. I've got a new bed and sofa coming on Monday evening. I'll be fine.'

'If you say so.' She shrugged, not quite be-lieving him, and headed back into the house, wondering if she should feel hurt that he didn't want to stay, and telling herself not to be stupid. He'd always been independent and she wasn't going to change him. 'How about I get stuck in and clean the rest while you do the bedroom, then?'

They stopped at eight because the light was failing and they were both tired, but his bed-room was painted and the kitchen, cloakroom and both bathrooms were gleaming and she'd started on the windows.

He waited till she'd finished the pane she was working on, then took the cloth out of her hand. 'Come on, it's late, and you're working tomorrow. Why don't we pick up a takeaway?'

She gave him a tired smile. 'That sounds great. How does the bedroom look?'

'Bigger, and it's got that amazing view.'

'Just as well, as you don't have any curtains. Right, come on, we've got another long day tomorrow.'

'Are you sure you don't mind? I feel like I'm taking advantage of your good nature.'

'Don't be silly. I wouldn't offer if I wasn't happy.'

He wasn't sure about that. Beth had a heart of gold, a heart that he'd broken, even if only indirectly, by not making sure she couldn't get pregnant.

'You're a star,' he said, echoing James, and she shook her head.

'No, Ryan, I'm a friend,' she said simply, and her words brought a lump to his throat because while it was true, in a strange way she meant so much more than that to him and he didn't have the words to say so.

He didn't even think there *was* a word for what they were to each other, he just knew she was an indelible part of his life and always would be.

By the end of Saturday the place was transformed.

Once the paint was dry he'd pulled up the carpet in the sitting room, dining room and hall, and together they mopped and polished the wood block floor and stood back to admire it.

'Wow. You were right, Beth, it is gorgeous. Stunning.'

'I thought it would be. How about pots and pans and things, if you insist on moving in so quickly? And bedroom curtains, come to that.'

'Oh, I'm sure Mum's got some I can borrow. I don't need much for the kitchen, and there's a box in the pantry. There might be something in there worth salvaging.'

They went and had a look, and the answer was a maybe.

'I'll take the box home, sort through it and put anything worth having through my dishwasher and bring it back tomorrow, if you give me a key,' she said, so he loaded it into her car, locked the house and went back to hers for the third and final night.

Not that he'd have a real bed until Monday, but as he'd said, a roof was more than he'd had at times, and he'd be fine—and maybe better than fine. He might even sleep if she wasn't lying there in the next room, just on the other side of the wall...

'Morning!'

Beth turned and met his eyes with a smile, her heart skipping a beat at the sound of his voice.

'Morning. All ready for your first shift?'

'Yes, absolutely. It'll make a refreshing change from painting. That's just mind-numbing.'

She felt her mouth twitch and bit her lip. 'Be careful what you wish for. Did you get on OK yesterday? And did you sleep last night?'

He laughed softly and propped himself up against the central desk. 'Like a log, but I'm looking forward to my new bed. I'm all done with sleeping bags.'

'You could have stayed at mine again,' she reminded him.

'I know, but I didn't want to outstay my welcome and I know you well enough to realise you wouldn't tell me if I had. Thanks for the card and the house plant. The place looks almost civilised in a rather empty way.'

'You're welcome,' she murmured. 'I thought it needed cheering up a bit. I put the kitchen stuff in the pantry, too. It might come in handy. Here—your spare key. And talking of keys, has anyone given you a locker or anything?'

He slid the key into his pocket. 'No, and I could do with some scrubs, if you could point me in the right direction?'

She nodded, and spent the next ten minutes sorting him out. 'Right, is that everything you need?'

'Pretty much. Thank you. I'd better go and find James.'

'He's in Resus.'

He nodded, and she went back to work and left him to find his feet, but it wasn't long before they were in Resus together, working on a patient who'd been brought in after being knocked off his motorbike by a driver who hadn't seen him.

His left leg had an open fracture and the paramedics has splinted it, but it didn't look good and he was clearly in a lot of pain and his blood pressure was low.

'Right, someone cut his clothes off so we can have a good look please,' Ryan said swiftly. 'Can I have the FAST scanner, and a gram of TXA in an infusion, and I want X-rays of the skull and that leg. Leave the collar and helmet on for now. Hi, I'm Ryan, and I'm a doctor. Can you tell me what happened, Jim?'

While he spoke to Jim and the radiographer took the X-rays, Beth set up the tranexamic acid infusion to slow the bleeding while Ryan's gentle fingers checked the man's ribs, abdomen and pelvis.

His leg was tinged blue below the fracture, and Beth checked the pulses in his foot.

'No pedal pulse,' she told Ryan, and he nodded.

'OK. Jim, there's a problem with the blood supply to your foot, so I'm going to have to pull your leg straight to sort that out. I'm sorry, it's going to hurt for a moment but it should feel better afterwards. OK, are you ready, Beth? On three.'

He pulled it straight, checked the pulse and then left her to deal with splinting it while he went back to the abdomen, a frown on his face as he ran the ultrasound wand below the man's ribs.

'There's a shadow. I think he might have an encapsulated bleed.'

'Spleen?'

He shook his head. 'No. Left kidney, maybe. There's a lot of bruising on this side, so I suspect a blunt force injury. Give him another gram of TXA as a bolus and let's get an X-ray of these ribs, and can we catheterise him, please, and check the urine for blood?'

She was already on it, and it proved his diagnosis right. The blood was obvious, and their patient was starting to deteriorate, so he was whisked away to Interventional Radiology for embolisation of the bleeding vessels before the orthopaedic surgeon could deal with his leg fracture.

They watched him go, and Ryan shook his head, a slightly bemused expression on his face as he stripped off his gloves and apron and headed for the sink.

'It feels odd not to finish the job. I would have had to deal with both of those injuries in the field, but at least we got the pulse back to his foot and he hasn't got a skull fracture, so it's all good.'

'You almost sound as if you wanted to do it all yourself,' she said, but he laughed and shook his head.

'No way. I'm happy to hand him over. I've had enough of juggling too many balls. They get dropped, and anyway, it's nice to have time for coffee occasionally. And that'll teach me to say the *c* word,' he said, and she looked up and saw the next patient already being wheeled in.

It set the tone of the day, one case piling on top of another, but he worked fast and thoroughly, and it was a joy to her to be working alongside him again. It gave her a chance to study him, to remember all the little things she'd forgotten, like the way he frowned when he was concentrating, the way his brow cleared the second it was all under control, the quirk of a brow, the brief nod when he was happy with something.

'Right, go for lunch, both of you,' James said, and she realised it was after two. She'd been working alongside him since before eight, and they hadn't stopped for breath.

'Sandwich and a coffee?' she suggested, and he nodded.

'That would be great. I'm starving. Breakfast was a long, long time ago.'

But yet again it wasn't to be. Another patient came through the doors, one of three from a nasty RTC, but Jenny, her line manager, came in and relieved her, so she went to the café and picked up lunch for both of them and he ate his in a snatched quiet moment a while later, washed down by the now tepid coffee she'd brought back for him.

'I can see why I was needed,' he said with a wry laugh.

'Oh, you're certainly needed. Still think it's better than painting your house?'

His chuckle was dry and a little rueful. 'It's certainly more mentally challenging.'

'Oh, well, you've only got another three hours to go. What time's your furniture being delivered?'

'I said not before six, and I can't see me getting away before then so hopefully it'll be eight or something. Whatever. They said they'd let me know. Right, I'd better go back and reassess my patient. I'll see you later.'

Not much later, as it turned out.

He was in Resus with another emergency, gloved up and trying to assess a nasty scalp wound with an arterial bleed when his phone jiggled in his pocket.

'Could someone get my phone, please?' he asked, and one of the nurses delved in his scrub top pocket and held it up to him.

Damn. He stared at it and groaned. 'Can someone find Beth, please, if she's still here? I need to ask her a favour.'

'I think she is,' Jenny said. 'Although she shouldn't be.'

'No, I know that, but I saw her walk past ten minutes ago so she might still be around.'

The nurse who'd delved in his pocket came back with Beth a moment later, and she tipped her head on one side.

'Problem?'

'Just a bit. I need another favour. I've had a message from the delivery team. They've said they'll be there at five and there's no way I can leave before six and if it goes on like this I won't get away then. Is there any way you could let them in?'

'Sure. I should have gone off an hour ago anyway.'

'I know.' He sighed. 'I keep asking you favours—'

'Don't be ridiculous.' She held out her hand. 'Key?'

Damn. It was still where he'd put it a few hours ago.

'Right trouser pocket.'

Their eyes locked, and she looked hastily away and squirmed her hand under his plastic apron and into his pocket, groping for the keys while he tried really, really hard to keep his mind in check.

Not to mention his body—

'These them?'

'No. The loose one, the one you gave me back,' he said, and gritted his teeth again while she went back in and rummaged again, then returned the others.

'Do you want me to check everything's OK?'

'No. Just let them in, sign for it as unchecked, that's all. Well, unless it's obviously trashed in transit.' He gave her a rueful smile. 'Thank you, Beth. I owe you, big-time.'

'You do. Don't worry, I'm keeping a tab.'

He grunted, and she gave him a cheeky grin and left him to the spurting artery and his mounting guilt.

She'd spent days helping him, and now she was heading back to his house, waiting in for the furniture. And he was clock-watching, dividing his guilt between his new job and his old friend.

If that was what you could call her, the woman you'd had a brief affair with, who'd ended up giving birth to a baby whose heart was so compromised she'd been doomed from the moment of conception.

There had to be a better word than 'friend.' It was what she'd called herself when he'd thanked her for all her help, but she was so much more than that, their relationship so complicated, and he knew they'd be bound together for ever by the heartbreaking loss of their tiny daughter.

His chest squeezed, and he focused his attention on his patient and put Beth, their baby and his guilt out of his mind.

It was after eight before she heard the scrunch of tyres, and she gave the bedding a last swipe with her hand to straighten it, then opened the door.

'Beth, I can't believe you're still here!' he said instantly, his face hugely apologetic. 'I'm so sorry. I thought you'd be gone ages ago. Have they not come yet?'

'Yes, of course they have, they came at five. I've just been pottering and waiting for you. Jenny rang me so I knew you'd be late.'

'I didn't. Not this late, anyway, and there was no way I could leave.'

'No, I gather you had another really nasty

RTC with multiple casualties. Nice, gentle introduction on your first day.'

He snorted softly. 'Tell me about it. At least I was working with you, which made it significantly easier. So I assume everything was OK with the furniture?'

'Fine—lovely. Come and have a look.'

She opened the bedroom door, and he stopped in his tracks.

'They built the bed?'

'No, I did, because I didn't think you'd want to do it after such a hectic shift.'

He stared at her. '*You* did it? Wow. I didn't for a moment expect you to do that, Beth. Thank you.'

'It was easy,' she said, lying slightly because another pair of hands would have been hugely useful. 'Eight bolts and a few screws.' She waggled an Allen key at him. 'They even provided the technology.'

He gave a soft laugh, and hugged her.

'Thank you so much. I really wasn't expecting—'

She put her hand over his mouth, cutting him off. 'Hush. You've spent your life looking after people. I thought it was time someone looked after you a bit.'

He reached up and caught her hand, pressing a kiss into her palm before threading his fingers through hers.

'Thank you.'

His eyes were filled with a host of conflicting emotions, and she guessed he was just as confused as she was. And it really didn't help that there was a massive bed right beside them...

She retrieved her hand gently and stepped out of reach, ignoring the tingling in her palm. 'I hope I used the right bedding. It was new, but it was all I could find that would fit.'

'No, that's great, it's all there is,' he said, his voice unexpectedly gruff. 'Did the sofa come?'

'Yes, they unpacked it and the coffee table and took all the packaging away. It looks really good. Go and see.'

She followed him into the sitting room with a silent sigh of relief, and he sat down on the sofa, then swung his legs up and groaned contentedly. 'Wow. An actual sofa, long enough to lie on—and it's comfy. That's such a luxury.' He looked around and laughed softly. 'It looks almost homely, in a rather bare sort of way. And the floor's beautiful.'

He got to his feet, staring down into her eyes searchingly. 'Look, I could do with a shower, but I'm hungry, and if you haven't eaten yet, how about going out for something? Nothing fancy, just a pub—or we can go posh, if you like. Up to you.'

Her stomach rumbled, and she gave him a wry smile. 'Food's probably a good idea. I haven't even given it a thought but there's not a lot in my fridge. I was going shopping after work but I got slightly side-tracked.'

'Then I'm definitely buying you dinner,' he said firmly, the guilt back in his eyes. 'Go home, get changed while I shower, and I'll pick you up in half an hour. And work out where you want to go.'

She nodded, then on impulse went up on tiptoe and kissed his cheek. The brush of stubble against her lips sent a shockwave through her body, and she dropped back onto her heels and headed for the door, more confused than ever.

'See you in half an hour, then,' she said lightly, and walked out, letting out a quiet rush of breath.

Clearly her body hadn't forgotten him, then...

'Where to?'

'I thought the Harbour Inn?'

Really? He glanced at her, then away again quickly before she could read his expression. Of all the places to choose...

'If you like. It's nice and close.'

He headed down towards the little yacht harbour, to the pub where they'd had lunch nearly two and a half years ago, just before he'd kissed her for the first time and set the ball rolling.

He'd split up with Katie when he'd realised she was trying to get pregnant to stop him joining MFA, and Beth had been right there at the time, working alongside him in Theatre, intriguing him, tempting him—but when after a few weeks he'd asked her out she'd said no, holding him at arm's length because she didn't want a relationship.

Well, neither did he, not so soon after Katie, and maybe not for years, but that didn't make him a monk, and after a week when everyone in the Midlands seemed hell-bent on injuring themselves and they'd been trapped together in Theatre for countless hours, the tension simmering between them had reached breaking point.

He'd needed to get away, get out of the city and away from Beth, but by sheer co-incidence they'd both been scheduled for a long weekend off, so he'd put his cards on the table and asked her to go away with him. No strings, no commitment, no relationship, just a few days of adult fun by the seaside after the week from hell, and with any luck it'd get it out of his system.

If she'd said no it would have made life awkward, but frankly it had been awkward enough, so he'd had nothing to lose.

She hadn't. To his astonishment she'd said yes, so he'd booked a room in a posh spa hotel in Yoxburgh and picked her up on the Saturday morning with a tingling sense of anticipation. They'd been too early to check in, so they'd driven down to the harbour, found the little pub and had lunch, then gone for a stroll along the riverbank to kill time.

And then he'd lifted her down off the stile and kissed her.

She hadn't held him at arm's length then, and they'd spent most of the next two days in bed having the hottest sex he'd ever had in his life.

He parked the car, slammed the door on his thoughts and headed into the pub with Beth.

'It hasn't changed at all,' he murmured.

'No. I doubt if it's changed for decades.

All part of its charm, I guess. So, what are we having?'

'Fish and chips.'

She laughed at him. 'Well, that's healthy.'

'I don't care. You can have whatever you like, but after a day like today I need comfort food and calories.'

She gave a low chuckle, the sound running over his nerves like teasing fingertips, and his body leapt to life.

'I might have the baked cod with a salad,' she said, and then she tilted her head and looked at him. 'How's Jim? Any news?'

'Yeah, he's OK. They took out his left kidney, and he's got an ex-fix on his leg, but he's doing all right. He's alive, anyway.'

'Good. How about the RTC that held you up this evening?'

'Well, they all made it, which is a relief. It's never good to lose a patient on your first day.'

She chuckled again, and he gave her an answering smile, but hers faded and she studied him thoughtfully.

'It was good working together again,' she said, and he nodded slowly.

'Yes. Yes, it was. I'd almost forgotten how intuitive we are together. It was like you knew what I'd want without me asking, but then you always could read my mind.'

'Or maybe I'm just a good nurse and know my stuff.'

He arched a brow, and she pretended to scowl at him, her mouth puckering and making him want to kiss it.

He put his hands in the air, giving up the fight to hold back his smile. 'Sorry, sorry. You are a good nurse. Best I've ever worked with. Is that better?'

'Yes. Thank you.' Her smile was back, playing around her mouth and softening her eyes, and for a moment he had an overwhelming urge to lean over and kiss her—

'Fish and chips?'

He sat back, took a long, slow breath and looked up at their server.

'Yeah, that's mine.' And in the nick of time...

'Coffee? Unless you want to get back to your lovely new bed?'

He hesitated, then gave in, knowing it was foolish, knowing he was on a knife edge but unable to walk away.

'It'll keep another half hour. Coffee would

be lovely.' He cut the engine and followed her into her house. 'Anything I can do?'

'No, you're fine, go and sit down, I'll bring it through.'

So while she put the kettle on he wandered into the sitting room and closed the curtains, then sat down to wait for her, his eyes seeking out the little silver box as they always did, his heart heavy.

If they'd known before that weekend what was to follow, none of this would have happened, but of course they hadn't. They'd spent the next two months together in blissful ignorance, and then in late January MFA had sent him on his first posting.

No strings, he'd said, so he'd had no contact with her, which had been fine because he'd been too busy to think about anything else, but then he'd come back on leave in early May, and he'd discovered she was pregnant.

It was his worst nightmare, the last thing he'd ever wanted to hear, and his first instinct was anger because he thought she'd done it on purpose, but then she told him their baby girl had such hugely complex congenital heart defects that she was unlikely to make it to term, and his world fell apart.

He was still reeling with shock when they lost her at twenty-seven weeks, the child he hadn't even known about until the week before. The child he hadn't wanted—or hadn't known he wanted until it was too late. The child he would never have the chance to get to know because her little heart had given up the unequal struggle and stopped beating before he could meet her and tell her how much he loved her.

He'd spent two years trying to forget, but he knew now he never would.

He walked over to the little silver box and picked it up with infinite tenderness, nestling it in his palm, his other hand stroking it, needing to touch it, to touch her, to hold her again.

His poor, perfect, broken baby girl.

*Why?*

'Ry?'

He put the heart down gently, as if not to wake her, and walked into Beth's open arms.

'I'm so sorry,' he murmured gruffly, his voice a little ragged. 'Why did it happen, Beth? Did they ever find out?'

'No. They have no idea. They didn't find anything in the tests—no chromosomal abnormalities, no genetic links, nothing to indicate it was anything other than a fault in her embryonic development. Just a glitch. One of those things.'

She eased out of his arms and sat down, patting the sofa beside her.

'Come on, sit down and drink your coffee.'

He sat, but his eyes kept going back to the little heart and the pretty box beside it. Pandora's box...

She put her mug down and looked at him, her eyes searching.

'Do you want to look at it now?'

Could she read his mind? Maybe.

'I don't know.'

She got up again and went over to the box, bringing it back and putting it down on the coffee table, just out of reach. He could feel his heart beating, feel every thud against his ribs, taste the fear.

But fear of what? The contents of the box, or his own feelings? Maybe it was time to face them both.

He put his mug down and reached out, picking up the box and resting it gently on his knees. Like Pandora's box, once opened,

things could never go back to how they'd
been. Could he risk that?

He swallowed, sucked in a long, slow
breath and lifted the lid.

# CHAPTER THREE

IT WAS THE letter that finished him.

He was expecting the rest. The beautiful little box contained all the poignant things he'd tried to blank out, like the tiny, precious footprints the midwife had made for them, the photographs she'd taken of them together holding Grace, the blanket they'd wrapped her in as they'd held her for hours in their arms before they said goodbye.

But at the bottom of the box was a single folded sheet of paper, and he lifted it out and unfolded it, totally unprepared for what it was.

A letter, from Beth to her baby daughter.

*My darling Grace*
*I can't tell you how much I love you,*
*how much I miss you every single day,*
*with all my heart. But you'll always be*

*part of me, and you're with me wherever I go.*

*Carrying you in my body for your short life, giving birth to you, holding you in my arms, was an honour and a privilege I will never forget, and I'm so grateful I had that chance.*

*You are the best part of me, and I will treasure you forever.*
*Sleep tight, my darling.*
*Mummy xxx*

The words swam in front of him, and she took the letter gently from his nerveless fingers and replaced it in the box with all the other precious things, then gathered him in her arms and held him while the racking sobs tore him apart.

She said nothing, just held him and rocked him, and gradually the pain subsided, leaving him feeling oddly cleansed, as if he'd been wiped clean.

Except not, because Grace's name, her footprints, her photo, and the memories they'd made that day were engraved on his heart, an indelible part of him just as they were of Beth, and it felt right.

She handed him tissues, then said gently, 'I guess that's been a long time coming.'

He gave a ragged, fractured laugh and met her eyes, tender with understanding. 'I guess so. I'm sorry.'

'Don't be. It's OK to cry. I can't begin to tell you how much I've cried for her.'

He swiped the tears off his cheeks again with the palms of his hands and shook his head to clear it. 'I haven't, though. I haven't let myself. That's why I didn't want to see. I suppose I've been in denial, really, ignoring it, but it didn't work, because it's always been there, deep inside, gnawing away at me like acid. It's odd. It doesn't feel like that any more. I'm sad, of course I'm sad, and I guess I always will be, but it's like a weight's lifted—does that make sense?'

She nodded. 'It makes absolute sense. It's acceptance, Ry. It takes a while to get there, but it makes it easier. You'll still have bad days, though, times when things bring it all back and it catches you on your blind side.'

He nodded and leant back, wrapping an arm around her shoulders and holding her as they sat there quietly together. They didn't speak, but for the first time he let himself think about the events of that day, the day their daughter had been born.

He thought about her delivery, how hard it had been all night knowing that at the end of it they would have nothing but memories. They'd induced her, because Beth didn't want to wait, and she'd refused all pain relief, wanting to feel every last moment of it because it was the last thing she could do for her daughter, so he'd been there for her, supporting her as well as he could while his heart felt as if it had been locked in ice.

It had been a long night, and then as the first fingers of dawn crept over the horizon and touched the sky with gold, the midwife lifted Grace's tiny body tenderly into Beth's waiting arms.

He'd stood there helpless in the deafening silence, the silence that should have been filled with a baby's cries, feeling as if he had no place there, no role in the tragedy, no way of making it better, but he'd been unable to leave them and so he'd stayed, eyes dry and gritty with exhaustion, his body as tight as a bowstring, his heart numb while Beth wept silent tears and spoke softly to her daughter.

And then she'd placed the baby in his arms, and his heart had cracked in two. It was the first and last time he'd cried for her, until tonight, and even then he hadn't really let go.

A week later they'd gone together to register her birth and death, and then they'd held a quiet funeral service for her. Three days later he'd been recalled for his next posting by MFA and she'd told him to go, so he'd gone, relieved to be able to escape the all-consuming grief and get on and do something useful that would help someone somewhere, even though he couldn't help her or himself.

Except of course there had been no escape, just a fierce suppression of his emotions until he'd become so used to it he'd thought he was over it.

Apparently not. Not by a long way.

He broke the silence at last, needing to acknowledge what she'd been through and his guilt for leaving her to deal with it alone. 'I'm so sorry I wasn't more help. I don't know how you did it—how you were so strong, so brave, through all of it.'

'I wasn't brave, Ry, not at all. I was just doing what had to be done, and then once it was done I just felt empty.'

'I shouldn't have left you.'

She took his hand and kissed it, then held it in her hands, warm and firm and kind, Beth all over.

'I sent you away, Ryan. I couldn't deal with your grief as well as mine, and that was wrong. We should have grieved together for our daughter, but we didn't know each other well enough. We still don't, but we're learning, day by day, and we'll get there.'

He nodded slowly. 'Yeah, I suppose so.' He glanced at his phone and sighed. 'Beth, I'm sorry, I need to go. It's after eleven and I'm sure tomorrow will be just as long as today.'

She chuckled softly. 'No doubt. I'm on a late, but you need to get to bed. You've had a hectic few days, you must be exhausted.'

'I am. I tell you what, that bed had better be comfortable,' he said wryly. 'Did you try it?'

'No, I didn't have time, but if it isn't there's always the sofa. At least you know that's comfy.' She cocked her head on one side, her eyes searching his. 'Are you all right, Ry?'

He laughed softly and nodded. 'Yes, Beth. I'm all right. You?'

Her smile was sad. 'I'm all right. I'm used to it now. It's the new normal.'

He nodded, wondering how long it would

take him to reach that point. He got to his feet, pulled her up and into his arms and hugged her gently.

'Thank you. Thank you so much, for everything. You've been amazing, ever since I got here. You've always been amazing.'

'Don't be silly.'

'I'm not. I mean it. You're the strongest person I know, Beth, and the kindest, and I don't deserve you. Thank you.'

She hugged him back, then let him go. 'You're welcome. I hope you sleep well.'

He laughed. 'I'm sure I will.'

She walked him to the door and he turned and kissed her, just the slightest brush of his lips on hers, and let himself out and drove home, then paused a moment on the drive, staring up at the stars twinkling in the clear, dark night, just as he had everywhere he'd been sent by MFA.

He loved the stars. They never changed, untouched by all the madness around him, the one constant in a changing world, and they never failed to centre him and put everything back into perspective.

*How small and insignificant we are...*

He let himself in, checked his email and looked at the bed—his new bed, carefully put together by Beth to save him the trouble because that was the kind of person she was—and felt another wave of guilt for leaving her alone when she'd been so sad and lost and torn with grief.

She would never have left him. He knew that, but at the time she'd been adamant that she didn't need him. Only now it turned out she had needed him, but she'd been unable to cope with his grief, too, because they didn't know each other well enough to grieve together.

Well enough to make a baby, but not well enough to lose one. Maybe, given time, they would find that closeness and with it some closure. He hoped so.

He looked at the bed again, but tired though he was he wasn't ready, so he made himself a cup of chamomile tea and went out into the garden, sitting on the steps where they'd sat together only a couple of days ago, Beth's letter to Grace echoing in his head.

Should he do the same? Write down his thoughts about his tiny daughter, the child he hadn't known he wanted, and add them to hers? All the milestones they'd miss, the tears, the tantrums, the laughter? Her first smile, her first tooth, her first step—

He heard a noise behind him, a slight scrabbling, rustling noise. A hedgehog, probably, or a fox. They were on the edge of farmland, so it wasn't unlikely.

And then he heard a whimper, and turned to see something creeping towards him across the grass. Something large, much bigger than a hedgehog, less shy than a fox.

A dog?

'Hello, sweetie. What are you doing here?' he asked softly, and it moved closer.

A dog. Definitely a dog, and not a small one, its tail wagging tentatively, black nose gleaming in the moonlight. He held out his hand, careful not to meet its eyes so it didn't feel threatened, and the dog crept closer, flicking out its tongue to lick his fingers. He turned his hand over and scratched its chin, and it wriggled closer—close enough for him to smell it.

Dog, river mud and who knew what else.

It whined, and he stroked the tangled, scruffy head that pressed into his hand, its ears scarcely visible under the matted hair.

'Oh, poppet. What a mess you're in. Who are you? What are you doing here?'

It crept closer still, until it was resting up against his hip, its head heavy on his lap, and his hand slid down and felt ribs sticking out, and the bumps of its spine. It must be starving. 'Are you hungry? Is that the matter?'

The dog got to its feet, tail wagging, and he got up and headed inside, the dog running ahead through the sitting room door to leap onto his brand new sofa.

'Hey! No! Get off that!'

It wagged its tail, tongue lolling, still on the sofa as if it owned it, and everything fell into place.

He let out a rueful laugh. 'You live here, don't you? This is your house.'

The tail thumped, and he shook his head.

'Get off my sofa. I don't care how cute you are, you stink and you're covered in mud. Come here, let's find you some food and then work out what to do with you.' He headed into the kitchen, and the dog followed, standing up on its back legs and peering at the worktop hopefully, tail lashing.

'Dog! You have absolutely no manners! Sit!'

Paws dropped to the floor, and the dog sat and whined at him pitifully. He tried hard not to laugh, and pulled open the pantry to find the things he'd raided from his mother yesterday.

'Right, what have we got here? Tuna. Do you like tuna? I guess you like anything. Tuna sandwich? Yup? Just don't tell the vet.'

He drained the spring water off the tuna and mashed it between two slices of wholemeal bread, and then chopped them roughly, put them in a bowl Beth had found in the box and dumped it on the floor.

'Well, that went down OK,' he said with a chuckle, and shook his head slowly. 'Dog, you need a bath, and a serious haircut. You're the scruffiest thing I've ever seen.'

He put some water down in another bowl, but after a couple of slurps it gave up and came back to him, wuffing hopefully.

Still hungry. He had some ridiculously expensive peanut butter with no added anything, so he smeared a little dollop on another bit of bread and gave it to him. Her? He didn't even know, but that was the least of his worries.

The smell, however...

He called Beth.

'I'm sorry to disturb you. Are you still up?'

'Yes. What's the matter? Is the bed awful? Don't tell me it fell to pieces—'

'I haven't got that far. Do you have any

very mild shampoo and conditioner? And a brush you don't care about, and a pair of scissors with blunt ends? Oh, and a hair dryer. And old towels. Lots of them.'

He heard a slightly choked noise, like a strangled laugh. 'OK, what's going on?'

'You know the house smelt of dog? Well, it's come back.'

'The smell?'

'No—well, yes, but on the dog. The dog came back, I have no idea where from, but whoever it belongs to, it's in urgent need of a bath. I think it's been in the river.'

She chuckled. 'I'll be right round.'

'I'm glad you think it's funny. Wear something scruffy.'

He heard another laugh as the line went dead, and he slid his phone into his pocket with a smile on his face and turned back to the dog, just in time to see it sneaking back onto the sofa, a stolen banana in its mouth…

'Oh, my word.'

'You have a habit of walking in here and saying that,' he said drily, and she chuckled and eyed him up and down.

'Well, you are covered in mud. So where is it?'

'In the conservatory. I had to banish it. It jumped on the sofa with a banana it stole off the side in the kitchen.'

She felt her eyes widen. 'Your new sofa, that you haven't even sat on for more than ten seconds?'

His mouth quirked. 'That's the one.'

She bit her lips, trying really, really hard not to laugh. 'Oh, dear. Good job it's leather, at least it'll wipe clean. Well, let's see this thing, then.'

'This thing' turned out to be a clump of tangled, matted fur on gangly legs, but one swipe of its tongue on her outstretched hand and she was smitten.

'Oh, dear. You are really, really muddy, poppet. I wonder what colour you are?'

'Goodness knows. I have no idea where to start.'

She laughed and shoved up her sleeves. 'Water, I think. A lot of water. Have you got a plastic jug or bowl or something we can mix the shampoo in?'

It took an hour, but finally the dog was bathed, then bathed again, and it turned out to be a dull, creamy grey, although that might have been the remnants of the river mud.

They cut the matted hair away around its ears and neck, and then turned their attention to its body.

'Well, little lady, you're a girl,' he said softly, clipping clumps off carefully around her armpits as she lolled on her back in the kitchen, tongue hanging out and all but grinning at him. 'I wonder what your name is, you tatty old thing?'

He sat back on his heels, studied the dog for a moment and grinned. 'Tatty. Perfect. And we can always call you Tatiana if we're trying to be posh.'

*We? Where had that come from?*

'You don't need to name her, Ryan. You don't even know whose she is,' Beth pointed out gently, and he felt a sudden sense of anticlimax.

'No. No, you're right, I don't,' he said, coming down to earth with a bump. 'I wonder if she's microchipped?'

'The neighbours might recognise her. Have you met any of them yet?'

'No, not yet,' he said, looking up from his clipping to meet her eyes. 'I haven't really had a chance.' He looked down into the dog's trusting eyes and sighed. 'And you're right, I don't need to give her a name because I can't keep her, can I? Even if she does think I've bought a new sofa especially for her.'

It was an odd thought, and he wasn't sure he liked it, but he had to be realistic. How could he keep her? He worked ridiculous hours and he lived alone. It simply wasn't fair.

But then she licked his hand, and his heart wrenched.

'You can't, Ry.'

He looked up at the softly voiced words. 'Can't what?'

'Keep her. You can't keep her.'

He stroked the damp head with its appalling haircut, looked into the melting dark eyes and felt like a traitor.

'Let's worry about that tomorrow,' he said hastily. 'For now, I have to find her somewhere to sleep, and you need to go home.'

He got to his feet, walked her to the door and hugged her hard.

'Thank you so much,' he mumbled into hair that smelt vaguely of river mud. 'I couldn't have done that on my own.'

'Don't thank me. It's not like it's your dog.'

That pang again.

'Yeah, you're right, although I'd stake my life she belongs to the tenants. She needs to to get rid of the occasional whiff of river mud that was coming from somewhere, dressed in jeans and a top that didn't matter, and headed for Annie and Ed Shackleton's house.

They lived just round the corner on the seafront, and it was the school holidays so hopefully they'd be in. She pulled up outside their house just as Annie was walking back with their dog, Molly, and she got out of the car with a smile.

'Morning, Annie. That was perfect timing!'

'Hi, Beth. Are you OK? What can I do for you?'

Ten minutes later, armed with a collar and lead and an appointment with the Shackletons' vet, Beth collected Tatty from Ryan's conservatory and was about to load her into the car when a voice came from behind her.

'She came back, then. I did wonder if she might.'

Beth turned round and saw an elderly man peering through the hedge. 'Oh—hi. Do you know her?'

'Yes, she belonged to the tenants. Said they were rehoming her but they looked a bit shifty about it. Did a runner in the middle of the night, too. Packed up a van and went.

go to the vet to see if she's microchipped. Goodness knows when I'll fit that in.'

'I can do it. I don't start work until tomorrow lunchtime. If you give me the key again I can pick her up and take her.'

'I don't know any vets. I don't know any anything here. I wouldn't know where to start.'

'I'll ask Annie Shackleton. They've got a dog, she'll tell me everything I need to know.'

He shook his head, then gave in, because something needed to be done with the dog, whatever. 'Here—the spare key. You might as well keep it,' he said, suppressing the thought that it felt vaguely symbolic. 'I'll leave her in the conservatory when I go, so if you could put her back there afterwards that would be great. There's nothing there she can trash. You'll need a collar and lead to take her, though, if your friend's got one.'

'I'll sort it. Get to bed. We'll be fine. I'll see you at twelve when my shift starts, and tell you what the vet said.'

He searched her eyes, then nodded and bent his head to kiss her, just as she came up on tiptoe to do the same to him. Their lips clashed, held, and he felt fire shoot through his body. The kiss deepened, changed from an accidental clash to a very deliberate but tender caress that came out of nowhere and didn't seem to want to end.

He wasn't sure who backed away first, but she turned and opened the door and let herself out hurriedly with a little wave, and he watched her go, his emotions in turmoil, his body screaming in protest.

The dog whined at his side, and he dropped his hand down and found her head. 'She's gone, sweetheart,' he said regretfully. 'It's time for bed. Come on, Tatty. Let's find you a bed and put you away for the night. I need some sleep because I've got to be at work in five hours.'

Haha.

Between the kiss and the dog howling and whining in the conservatory there was no way he was going to sleep, so after two hours he relented and let her in, spread one of his new bath towels on the floor beside the bed and pointed firmly at it.

'Down!'

She gave him a baleful look, curled up on it and stayed there, to his relief, and he finally managed to drop off.

For a while, at least, but when his alarm

dragged him up to the surface at six she was there, lying up against him on the bed, her head next to his on the pillow.

He turned his head and glared at her. 'Tatty, you can't do this! Off!'

No chance. She grinned and licked his face, and he wondered just exactly when, if ever, she'd been wormed. He threw the covers off and got up, heading for the bathroom with the dog at his heels.

'You need the vet, and I need a shower and some clothes that don't smell of you, because I have to go to work. Do you want breakfast first? Probably.'

She polished off the rest of his loaf of bread, mostly while his back was turned, and she didn't even have the grace to look guilty.

He put her back in the conservatory and went to work hungry.

Poor Ryan.

The look on his face when he'd realised he couldn't keep her. Still, maybe by this morning he'd thought better of it. He'd probably thought better of their goodnight kiss, at least. She certainly had—hadn't she?

*Liar.*

She got up, showered and washed her hair

I reckon they owed rent again. So, you and your young man have taken it on, have you?'

For a moment she wasn't sure if he was talking about the house or the dog, but then she realised he was looking at the house. 'Yes—well, Ryan has. He's not my young man, he's just a friend.'

*Why did that feel like a lie?*

The man pushed his way through a gap in the hedge, and stuck his hand out. 'I'm Reg, by the way.'

She freed a hand from the lead and shook his. 'I'm Beth.'

Reg stooped and patted the dog. 'He's brave taking it on. They left it in a right old state.'

'Yes, they did, but it's better now. Reg, I'm sorry, I don't want to be rude but I've got an appointment with the vet.'

'Better not hold you up then, young lady. Nice to meet you. And tell your Ryan if there's anything he needs, just ask.'

'I will.'

He gave the dog a last pat and she watched him wrestle his way back through the gap in the hedge, then she opened the boot and gave Tatty a little tug. She sat down and whined, and Beth eyed her thoughtfully.

She was NOT a small dog. The boot was barely big enough. Did she *really* need to wrestle with her?

'Please, Tatty. Come on. Good girl,' she wheedled, and to her astonishment the dog jumped in, licked her hand and sat down.

Phew. She got behind the wheel and drove carefully to the practice, one eye on the rear-view mirror, but the dog just sat there, giving the odd whine. Presumably her last journey had ended in her being evicted from the car and dumped in the middle of nowhere—unless she genuinely had been rehomed and had simply run away?

'Poor Tatty,' she said softly, and the dog whined again.

'Well? Do we know who she is?'

'Sort of. No microchip, as expected, but I met your neighbour, Reg. She was the tenants' dog.'

He nodded. 'I was pretty sure she was. She made herself at home last night, anyway. She ended up on my bed.'

Beth's eyes widened, and he laughed.

'Don't look surprised. She's very persuasive when she's howling at three in the morning and I didn't want to be kicked out by the landlord.'

'I don't think that's going to happen. After the last lot, he's going to be only too happy to have you there. Reg said if there's anything you need, just ask, by the way. He seemed to think we were a couple. I told him you were just a friend.'

That word again. Even less right after their kiss last night. He grunted. 'I'll go and introduce myself when I get home. So did he say what the dog's name was?'

'No, but I didn't ask, and the vet didn't recognise her, but apparently she's possibly some kind of retriever cross, she's young, and there's something else you need to know. She's about four or five weeks pregnant.'

He felt his jaw drop, and sighed and rolled his eyes. 'Seriously? Oh, Beth. What the hell do we do now?'

'We?' She laughed and walked away. 'Your dog, McKenna. It's nothing to do with me. I suggest you try and contact the owners.'

Over his dead body.

But realistically, did he have a choice? He rang the letting agent, told him the dog had come back and asked if he had a forwarding address for the previous tenants, but of course he didn't. They owed two months' rent. Why would they give anyone their address?

Which left him with the need to rehome her somehow. He found a rescue centre on the internet, and the moment he got home he rang them.

They were full, but they said they'd take her as soon as they had a space.

'Don't hold your breath, though,' the receptionist said. 'It could be a while. Are you able to keep her in the meantime?'

He said he could, trying to work out why the feeling in his chest felt remarkably like relief, then gave her his details and went into the kitchen and found a note from Beth, propped up against the kettle.

*Dry food's in the pantry. She's twenty-five kilos but add twenty per cent more food because she's pregnant. Couldn't find scales, but she's had lunch and didn't seem to mind! Chart on the side of the food bag. Divide by three—obvs. And keep the door shut!*

He sighed, went into the pantry with Tatty at his side, and examined the chart with a bit of enthusiastic assistance. Beth hadn't been able to find the scales because there weren't any, but he made an educated guess.

That would do, for now. He'd give her a bit more later and buy scales tomorrow. Assuming he'd still have her. Sounded like it.

He put her dry food into the bowl Beth had left him, ate a tin of baked beans cold out of the can with a fork, and looked at the clock on the cooker.

Quarter to eight. Still time for a quick walk before dusk, if they didn't hang about. He put Tatty—no, the dog—on the borrowed lead and took her down to the river and along the river wall. She didn't seem keen on the lead, but she seemed happy enough by his side and soon got used to it, and they walked until the light was fading and got home just before nine.

He was still hungry, but of course she'd eaten the bread that morning so he couldn't even make a sandwich, so he had a bowl of cereal and gave the dog another handful of kibble, then made a coffee and headed for the sitting room, the dog in tow.

All he wanted was to sit down quietly on

the sofa with his phone, check his emails and do a little research into dog pregnancy and rehoming—although if he was rehoming her, the pregnancy research was irrelevant.

Assuming he got a chance to do it anyway, because Tatty had gone in the garden and come back victorious with a muddy ball in her mouth, and dropped it at his feet.

Of course. Somewhere in her ancestry was a retriever. And all they wanted to do, like all the gun dog breeds, was just exactly that. So he rolled the ball, and she fetched it, and he rolled it, she fetched it, over and over again until finally he hid it behind his back.

'No. It's gone. Lie down.'

She whined, gave a resigned sigh and hopped onto the sofa, curled up and went to sleep. Well, almost. One eye was still slightly open, just in case…

He grunted and turned his attention back to his dog-rehoming research.

# CHAPTER FOUR

'How's Tatty?'

'The *dog* is clingy. And needy. And playful. Endlessly playful. Not to mention greedy in the bedroom. I bought a six-foot-wide bed because I like space, and she's claimed at least half of it.'

Beth suppressed a smile. 'You could buy her a basket.'

He made a noise somewhere between a grunt and a snort, and rolled his head on his neck. It crunched and made her wince.

'Ouch.'

'Oh, it doesn't hurt, it's just stiff from hanging off the edge of the bed half the night. I met Ed Shackleton, by the way. We were out on the river wall by six this morning, and so was he, and he recognised her. He stopped me and introduced himself and asked how she was, so I told him. He laughed.'

He said it deadpan, but his lips were twitching and she had to bite hers. 'He laughed?'

'Yes. Apparently he thinks it's funny. She and Molly made friends.'

'Did you let her off the lead?'

A definite snort this time. 'No. I have better things to do with my early morning than look for a dog that's messed off and won't come back.'

'I thought she was clingy?'

'Would you rely on that? Anyway, Ed said Annie could pick the dog up on her walk with Molly and take them both, and give her some lunch, so I gave him the key to the back door. At least I don't have to worry about that today. So, what's going on this morning?' he asked, turning his attention back to the day job, and she ran through the weirdly short list of patients on the whiteboard.

'That looks pretty quiet. Excellent. I might sneak off for a proper, decent coffee. I haven't got my coffee-maker out of store yet—'

'Adult trauma call, five minutes. Paediatric trauma call, five minutes.'

He tilted his head and glared at the speaker on the wall.

'Seriously? I need a coffee first!'

She grinned at him. 'Poor baby. You can get one later. Come on. Last one in Resus buys lunch.'

Lunch? What was that again?

He ignored his whinging stomach, and finally, sometime after three, there was a gap. An actual, time-for-a-break gap.

Hallelujah! He grinned at Beth.

'Coming for lunch?'

'Absolutely. And you're buying.'

'My pleasure. Let's just get out of here before the red phone bursts into life again. Are you always this short-staffed?'

'No, it's the Easter holidays. Andy Gallagher's technically only part-time, but he's picked up a lot of the slack until you arrived and they've got five children, so he's having time off in lieu now, and Sam Ryder's wife's sick so he's off with the kids, and when Andy comes back James is off for a week. And two of the nurses with kids are off as well, so it's worse than usual.'

'I'm glad to hear it. I can't imagine what it's like at Christmas.'

She gave a slightly hysterical laugh and pushed open the café door.

'Trust me, you don't want to know.'

He picked up a tray and slid it along the counter, peering at the range of salads on offer. He really, really needed to do an internet food order—

'So have you applied for the job yet?'

He rolled his eyes. '*Et tu, Brute?* I've had James on my case all morning.'

'So, are you going to?'

He picked up a bowl of mixed salad, added a dollop of coronation chicken and dumped it on the tray with a bread roll and a banana. 'I guess—if I ever have a minute. The dog's taking up a lot of my time.'

She put her salad down on the tray beside his. 'I thought you were going to re-home her?'

'They're full. All of them. I did some ringing round.'

'Ah.'

'Indeed. Black Americano, please, with an extra shot. Beth?'

'Oh—skinny cappuccino, please. So what are you going to do?'

He stared blankly at the back of the barista. 'Honestly? I don't know. Technically, she's not my problem.'

'But?'

He laughed softly, took the coffees, picked

up the tray and paid, then headed out into the park to find a table.

'But?' she repeated. She raised an eyebrow at him and waited, and he gave a resigned sigh.

'What can I do? Dammit, Beth, the dog's pregnant! I can't just kick her out. That would make me no better than them. Oh, she was called Dolly, by the way.'

'*Dolly?*'

He laughed. 'Exactly my reaction. Anyone less like a doll… Tatty suits her a lot better, but according to Reg, the kids used to carry her around in their arms when she was a puppy.'

Her face crumpled slightly. 'Oh, they must miss her.'

'Yeah. I reckon she misses them, too. She keeps going into the other bedroom as if she's looking for them. Whatever. I'm sure the rescue centre can find her a good family, when they've got room.'

He took a mouthful of food, but it stuck in his throat, lodged on top of a strange lump that had appeared. He swallowed hard, took a gulp of coffee and burnt his mouth.

Livvy Henderson smiled at them and walked past, waving at a man sitting at a table beyond them. He'd met the ED registrar last week when Beth had asked her about the house she'd rented, and he'd worked with her a couple of times since. He followed her with his eyes as she bent over and kissed the man, then sat beside him as he put his arm around her.

'Who's that with Livvy?' he asked, pretending interest to change the subject.

'Matt Hunter, consultant trauma surgeon. You're bound to meet him. He's her fiancé. They're getting married in a few weeks—at our hotel, actually.'

His eyes flicked back to hers, then away again, his heart pounding as his mind was dragged back to their weekend.

'Good venue,' he said calmly. *So much for changing the subject. Be careful what you wish for...*

'Yes, it is. Actually, there's something I want to ask you. I've got an invitation to the evening do. I don't suppose you fancy being my plus one? I don't really want to go on my own, and I know you aren't going to get any ideas if I ask you.'

He stifled a snort. He wasn't so sure about that, especially not in the hotel that had so many X-rated memories. And besides, he thought most weddings were outrageously lavish, absurdly expensive and he'd never understood the need to squander that much money on what amounted to a party.

Not that Katie had agreed about that, but then it turned out that they hadn't agreed on much. He'd been very clear that he didn't want to get married or have children any time soon because he really wanted to work with Medicine For All, and he thought she'd understood. When he realised she'd stopped taking her contraception and was quietly planning a wedding, he'd put his foot down, and it had finally dawned on her that he wasn't just saying it and she couldn't talk him round, or talk him out of his plans to sign up with MFA.

She'd had a screaming fit, said she wouldn't stay with him unless he backed down, so he said fine, told her to go and walked out.

Cue all kinds of fallout, underpinned by a certain amount of guilt, a tinge of regret and a huge sense of relief on his part when it turned out that she wasn't yet pregnant. That was just before he'd started working with Beth, and why he'd wanted a no-strings non-relationship with her, something light-hearted and physical and without any kind of commitment from either of them.

So much for light-hearted, given their fated pregnancy and the emotional turmoil it had left in its wake. After his initial furious reaction that she'd done it on purpose, the way Katie had tried to, came the gut-wrenching knowledge that their baby was dying, which had tapped into something deep inside him, a paternal urge he hadn't even known existed. Something he still, even now, couldn't really understand and wasn't sure he was ready for.

And going back to the hotel where it had all started wasn't in any way on his agenda. Emotions aside, he was finding working with her distracting enough and his libido was running riot.

'Are you sure there isn't someone else you could go with? You know I don't really do weddings.'

'I take it that's a no, then?' she said, her voice light but her eyes guarded, with a tinge of hurt lurking in their depths.

Dammit. He gave up fighting. 'When is it?'

'Four and a bit weeks. The eleventh of May,' she added softly, and he felt as if a bucket of ice had been tipped over him. 'It's—'

'I know what day it is,' he said gruffly.

Exactly two years to the day since Grace's heart had stopped beating, and she'd been born the next day, the date engraved on the little silver heart. And on his, and Beth's, too, he had no doubt.

Such bitter irony, that the wedding should be on that day, of all days, and in that venue, of all the venues they could have chosen.

How could he not go, just because he *didn't do weddings*? Not even he was that selfish and self-centred.

He nodded. 'OK. I'll come. What's the dress code?'

Not that it mattered a jot. He'd go in a bin bag if necessary, because there was no way he'd leave her alone on Grace's anniversary, no matter how little he wanted to be there.

'Black tie. Livvy wanted black tie because she said Matt looks so good in a DJ.'

He grunted, searching in his head for where the hell he might have stored his DJ. His mother's wardrobe? There was still some stuff there. Or he could buy a new one. He was thinner now, the old one might not fit any more. Whatever, he had a month to sort it out.

'Problem?' she asked, her eyes troubled, and he smiled at her and shook his head.

'No, Beth. It's not a problem. I just can't remember where I've put my DJ, but that's fine. I've got time to sort it. Unlike the dog. I don't know what to do about her. I can't leave her alone and unfed all day while I'm at work, but I just feel stuck with her.'

'I have an idea. Why don't you ask Reg if he could pop in at lunchtimes and let her out and feed her, just until the rehoming place can take her? He seemed to have a bit of a soft spot for her.'

He looked at her thoughtfully. 'Do you think he would?'

She shrugged. 'I don't know. He might. You could ask. And then you could stop worrying about her all day.'

'I don't.'

'Liar.'

Could she actually see straight through him?

He ate his salad, drank his coffee and met her eyes again. 'We need to get on.'

'We do. What are you doing later?'

He laughed. 'Walking the dog?'

'Can I come?'

On the river path, over the stile where

he'd kissed her that time? His heart crashed against his ribs in anticipation.

'Yes, of course.' Only this time he'd keep his hands to himself...

Beth put jeans and boots on, and drove round to Ryan's. She could have walked, it was only about five minutes away, but she knew he'd be in a hurry, and when she pulled up on the drive they were already there waiting. And Tatty seemed ridiculously excited to see her again.

'Hello, sweetie,' she crooned gently, rubbing Tatty's chest and earning herself a happy, doggy smile, and they set off across the lane through a gap in the hedge and along a footpath that led over the marshes to the river.

She fell into step beside him, their arms brushing as they walked. And somehow, she wasn't sure how, her hand ended up firmly wrapped in his. She knew how it had got there—she'd slipped on some mud, and he'd grabbed her—but then he hadn't let go, so they'd walked on, her fingers curled around his, his thumb over the top of hers, and every now and then it moved, a gentle, rhythmic stroke, or a little squeeze that made her feel warm inside.

They reached the river and went left, heading upriver for a while, then turned back towards the harbour nestled in the river mouth, retracing their steps as they had all that time ago.

He had to let go of her hand to steer Tatty round the stile, but then as she climbed over after him he held out his hand again, and their eyes met and held.

'This is where you first kissed me,' she said softly, and something hot and wild and a little dangerous to her peace of mind flickered in his eyes and was gone.

'I know.'

And then he let her go, and turned on his heel and walked on, Tatty hanging back to wait for her as she jumped down off the stile and caught them up, her heart fizzing in her chest.

It was still there, whatever *it* was, simmering between them like molten lava, and she felt a sudden surge of regret for asking him to go with her to the wedding. It was bound to be unashamedly romantic and inevitably they'd be expected to dance, and that would only complicate things, although how they could get more complicated it was difficult to see. Maybe he'd pull out, because right now he couldn't seem to get away from her fast enough.

He turned his head and looked at her, his expression neutral now. 'Fancy going to the pub again for supper?' he asked, and her eyes widened in surprise. She'd thought he was desperate to get home, but for some reason he wasn't. Had she read him wrong?

'What about Tatty? Will she behave?'

He shrugged. 'We could give it a try. Ed said they're dog-friendly, and I've got nothing at home because I still haven't done an internet order and lunch seems like a long time ago.'

It did, and she didn't have much food in her house, either. That had been a job for her way home, only her agenda had been hijacked again, by herself this time.

'Sounds lovely,' she said, summoning up a smile and wishing it didn't feel like a date. Too complicating. Too much, too soon.

But it wasn't a date and anyway she'd said yes now, so she followed him in, and they found a little table in the dog-friendly end of the bar, and Tatty lay down with her head on her paws and went to sleep.

'She's tired. I ought to take her to the vet and talk about this pregnancy.'

'I thought you were going to rehome her?'

He shrugged, his mouth pulling down at the corners in a wry grimace. 'I will, when I can. But in the meantime I need to know what to do for her.'

'What, apart from letting her sleep on your bed and dominate your every waking moment?'

The wry grin turned into a chuckle. 'That's the one. Still, I talked to Reg when I got home and he seems happy to let her out and feed her in the middle of the day, so it's not as urgent any more. Right, I'm starving. What are we going to eat?'

'Coming in for coffee?'

Beth hesitated, but he had a slightly guilty look in his eyes, as if he had an ulterior motive.

'I'd like your help,' he added when she didn't answer. 'Again.'

'With?'

'My job application. The closing date's Friday, and it's already Wednesday, and it needs some serious work. I haven't updated my CV recently, and—well, a lot's changed. There's all my aid stuff, and I've only got a basic CV for locum work. It's not nearly adequate for a consultancy.'

'So what do I know about it? It's James you need to talk to. He's so keen to have you he'll probably write your application letter for you if you ask him.'

She knew there was no way he'd ask him, but she left it hanging, and he shrugged.

'I think I can manage without doing that,' he said drily. 'And don't worry if you'd rather not, I'll be fine,' he added, obviously reading the reluctance in her eyes, but she relented and smiled at him.

'It's all right, I'll help you. You've bought me lunch and supper today, so it's the least I can do—and anyway, I haven't got anything else planned.'

'Thank you.' He returned her smile, opened the door and headed for the kitchen. 'I need to feed the dog, then I'll make some coffee.'

'I thought you didn't have coffee?'

He grinned at her. 'I don't, not bean to cup, at least, but I have got a cafetière and some ground coffee so I'm not entirely deprived.'

He disappeared into the pantry. 'Stick the kettle on,' he added over his shoulder, but she was already at the tap with it in her hand, staring across the marshes to the river path in the distance. She could just about make out the stile. Did he stand here looking at it like that?

Wondering how it had all happened, how something that was meant to be harmless fun had gone so wrong?

She put the kettle on its stand, her eyes drawn back to the stile, picked out on the horizon by the setting sun. There'd been a strange expression in his eyes today as he'd looked up at her on the stile, as if his feelings had bubbled close to the surface. She wondered what would happen if he set them free, and felt a shiver of anticipation.

'Tatty, sit.'

She dragged her eyes off the stile and turned to see the dog obediently sitting, her eyes fixed on the bowl, tail lashing back and forth across the worn-out tiles.

'Good girl,' he said, putting it down and giving the dog a little pat, and then he straightened up and met her eyes.

'What?'

Beth shrugged, suppressing a smile. 'Nothing.'

'I'm not going to be mean to her just because I can't keep her.'

'If you say so.'

He made that grunty, snorty noise that was becoming all too familiar as a punctuation point in their conversations, and then reached down two mugs and the cafetière, spooned coffee into the jug and poured water on it, releasing the aroma.

'Oh, that smells good. It'll probably keep me awake all night, though.'

'Want to change your mind?'

'No, I'll just hate you all night instead.'

'I'll get some decaf for you,' he promised with a chuckle, and picking up his coffee, he headed for the sitting room with Tatty in hot pursuit. He threw her off the sofa, sat down on one side and patted the other for Beth, pushed Tatty off again and opened his laptop.

'Right. Let's nail this CV.'

'I've got an interview on Tuesday.'

Beth glanced up from her patient notes and grinned at him. 'Well, there's a surprise. Did you get a letter?'

He shook his head. 'No. James just told me. They gave it a few days longer, but there's only been one other serious applicant and James thinks he's looking for a nice quiet seaside town to wind down into retirement.'

She felt her eyes widen. 'He told you that?'

'Off the record. Apparently he's got more experience than me—well, on paper he has, I'm sure, as he's older, but I've done a lot so maybe that'll balance it.'

He had. She'd seen his CV—she'd practically written it for him a week ago—and it was packed with a huge variety of things he'd seen and done. He might not have great depth of experience, but he certainly had breadth.

Which meant he was in with a good chance of getting the consultancy.

Which meant she was in with a good chance of having him here, in Yoxburgh, for the foreseeable.

Did she want that? Even now, not quite two weeks into their new—no, not relationship. That sounded like something else, something they definitely didn't have. Friendship, then. Two weeks into their new friendship, she still wasn't sure if she could live with him so near. So near and yet so far?

No. Friendship didn't say enough. They'd

been friends before, but this—this was different. This was life after Grace, and that changed everything, every aspect of their interaction with each other.

It was broader than a friendship, deeper than a physical relationship, more complicated than an ex-relationship but without its depth. Although they'd certainly plumbed the depths in their grief, if not together. And then there was that kiss last week, and the sizzling look he'd given her last week by the stile—

'Beth? Are you OK?'

She found a smile, contemplated lying and gave up. 'I was just trying to work out what we are to each other.'

His answering smile was wry, with a wealth of sadness that made her want to weep. 'I gave up trying to work that out days ago. I don't think there is an accurate definition, but at the very least, we're friends. Well, I hope we are.'

'Of course we are.'

'Good.' He gave her a gentle hug, then let her go, leaving a tidal wave of emotions in his wake. 'I'm needed in Resus. James had to do a thoracotomy in a field. Literally. A car overshot the junction, ripped through a barrier and cartwheeled down into a field. I gather it wasn't pretty.'

She winced. 'It doesn't sound pretty. How on earth did that happen in broad daylight?'

'I don't know. The driver was dead at the scene. He might have had a heart attack or a stroke—who knows. I think this is the front seat passenger coming in. I'll let you know more when I find out.'

'Good luck with it. I'm off to sort out an ingrowing toenail.'

'Sure you don't want to delegate and come and help me?'

She smiled and gave him a push towards Resus. 'Quite sure. I had enough of Resus at the weekend. Go on, shoo. I'll see you later.'

'Dinner at mine after a dog walk?'

She hesitated, and he frowned.

'Tatty misses you. She hasn't seen you for days.'

'Three days. I saw her on Sunday evening.'

He smiled coaxingly. 'That's a long time in a short life and you're on nights all over this coming weekend, so she'll hardly see you then. If I've even still got her,' he added in a blatant attempt at emotional blackmail, and she rolled her eyes.

'Oh, all right, I'll come for a dog walk

and dinner—now go!' He grinned, blew her a kiss and strode off, leaving her wondering how she'd given in so easily. And she'd been trying to keep him at a little more distance, too.

'Weak.'

'Who's weak?'

'Oh, hi, Livvy. Nobody. I'm just trying to work out how long I have to get an outfit for your wedding.'

'More than a week! Try three and a half.'

'Are you ready for it?'

She laughed. 'Emotionally, yes. Are all my ducks in a row? Probably not! Still, I've got Mum on the case. She'll pick up the slack, she always does. She throws the best parties. Did you want me to have a look at this ingrowing toenail? I hear it's pretty horrendous.'

His furniture arrived that weekend, delivered from the storage unit where it had all been lurking for over two years, but he'd given up trying to manage without it, even though he'd only been offered an interview for the permanent post and might well not get it. Still, previous or not, he needed some of the things he'd had in store, and in between shifts he spent the entire weekend trying to work out where to put it all. Not that he was going to unpack everything. Not yet.

His study was the last thing he needed to worry about, because he'd need bookshelves for all the endless boxes of books and notes and paperwork, so he stashed all study-related stuff in that room together with other things that he simply didn't need yet, if at all, and shut the door on it and tackled the rest.

That in itself was quite enough, and it was made worse by the fact that Beth had been working all weekend on nights, so he hadn't even been able to enlist her help.

Not that that was fair. He'd asked enough of her as it was and she'd been more than generous, and anyway, he was beginning to think he was just using the house as an excuse to spend time with her, so he ploughed on alone. Safer that way, because working with her was becoming a bit of a minefield, the tension starting to build again as it had before, but sorting the house alone was getting very, very dull.

He was contemplating the mess and tearing his hair out when she breezed in early on Monday afternoon, all smiles and bearing a carrier bag. She delved into it and pulled out a cake, and suddenly everything seemed doable.

'Oh, I love you,' he said fervently, and all but snatched the cake out of her hands.

'Hey! Where are you going with that?'

'The top shelf of the pantry until we get round to it. I'll make coffee first. My bean-to-cup machine arrived.'

'I can see that. Are you assuming it still works after being in storage?'

He laughed again, ridiculously pleased to see her. 'Are you kidding? It was the first thing I unpacked. It works—I've nearly worn it out in the last two days. So, what's it to be? Cappuccino?'

She smiled, her eyes crinkling at the corners and making him want to kiss her. 'Definitely. Oh, and while I think about it, you'd better put this in the fridge for later.'

She delved into the bag again and pulled out a bottle of something fizzy. 'I figured as you were properly moving in now and claiming it, at least for a while, we ought to christen it.'

'Ah, Beth, you're a sweetheart. Thank you! We'll definitely have it later.'

He took it from her, stashed it in the fridge

and pulled her into his arms for a brief hug, but she settled against his chest as if she belonged there, and it was a real struggle to let her go, because it just felt so *right*.

*No. Don't go there. Too messy, and you've done enough damage, and anyway, she doesn't want you.* He dropped his arms and stepped back.

'Right. Coffee and cake in the garden, then I've got a job for you.'

'You have? What a surprise. Go on, then, hit me with it.'

But she was smiling, so he relaxed and smiled back.

'Pictures. I'm going to put my old bed together for the spare room so my mother can come and visit me sometime, and I want you to look through the pictures and work out where they need to go. Not all of them, just the odd one here and there to make it feel like home. But first, cake.'

He didn't have a huge number of pictures, but there were a few she remembered, including one of a wild, rugged landscape that had hung over his bed, and it made her body tingle just to look at it.

How many times had they made love on

the bed beneath it? Dozens, every one of them memorable. She put it to one side and sorted through the others, the less contentious ones. Or less evocative, at least, of their past, the pre-Grace period before he'd gone away for the first time, when their lovemaking was smoking hot and nothing else was taken seriously.

He'd made her laugh, made her gasp with ecstasy and weep with frustration, but always, always, he'd set her on fire. It had been the perfect antidote to Rick's cheating and lying ways, and just what she'd needed. Intensely passionate, and yet light and frivolous—or it would have been if things hadn't turned out the way they had, but the heat, the passion, was still there smouldering under the surface, and it was getting harder and harder to ignore.

'I like this one,' she said, turning her head when she heard him behind her, and he nodded, coming right up close to look over her shoulder at the painting.

'I got it in a gallery in Cumbria when I was visiting my uncle shortly before he died, and I've never got round to hanging it. I just love the miles of flat sand and the distant sea. It all looks so harmless and peaceful, but look at the menace in the sky, and when that tide comes in…'

Like their relationship, which had seemed harmless enough, and would have been, if tragedy hadn't intervened. She sucked in a breath and looked away.

'Where do you want it?'

He shrugged. 'I don't know. On that wall, opposite the sofa?'

'Go and hold it up, then, let me look at it.'

She sat on the sofa, instantly joined by Tatty, and her hand found the dog's head and lay on it while she gave him directions.

'Right a bit—down—OK, hold it there. Have you got a pencil?'

'No. Come and take it from me and hold it here, and I'll find one.'

She squeezed under his arm and took it from him, all too aware of his body against her back, the closeness of his head to hers, the soft whisper of his breath against her hair.

'Stand back and have a look at it while you're at it, but be quick, it's heavy,' she said over her shoulder.

'Perfect. Right, keep still,' he said, and leant in against her, his arm coming round her to mark the bottom of the picture.

The back of his hand brushed against her

breast and she jerked, the frame knocking the pencil so it slid a little on the wall.

'Sorry—lost my grip,' she muttered, which wasn't far from the truth, although only in a metaphorical sense, and he backed away with a chuckle as she put the picture down.

'I wasn't trying to grope you, Beth.'

*Pity...*

'I didn't say you were. Want to try again?'

His eyebrows shot up, and she struggled to keep a straight face.

'Not that, idiot. The picture.'

His chuckle was infectious, and she got the giggles in spite of herself.

'Sorry,' she said, when she could speak again, but he just shook his head and pulled her into his arms and hugged her.

'Don't be. It's lovely to see you laugh, Beth. I've missed it.'

'I've missed it, too.' Missed him, missed his arms around her, missed his body entwined with hers. Missed lying in his arms afterwards, listening to his heart beat as she fell asleep. Missed all of it.

She smiled, a wonky little smile by the feel of it, and eased away from him. 'So, the picture.'

He looked at the mark on the wall and shrugged.

'That's good enough. I can hang it a fraction lower to cover it,' he said, his voice suddenly gruff, and she backed away, her legs like jelly, because the air was suddenly full of something wild and dangerous and totally not on her agenda. Or it shouldn't be.

He measured the wall, marked the centre, measured the height for the hook and banged it into the wall. Firmly.

'Right, how's that?' he asked, settling it on the hook.

'Good. Great,' she said without giving it a glance. 'So what else is there?'

'More coffee?' he asked, heading for the kitchen, and she followed him, her body still reeling from that accidental touch.

Stupid. It happened all the time at work when they were reaching round each other to get to the patient, so why did it feel so different now?

*Because we're alone, playing house, and it's all getting a bit real...*

'I fancy another bit of cake—going to join me?' she asked, and hoped her voice sounded normal, because the rest of her body certainly wasn't. It was clamouring for that wild and dangerous something she'd seen in his eyes, and she put the slice of cake on his plate and slid it towards him, picked up her own and retreated to the window, standing with her back to him while her body screamed at her to turn round, walk into his arms and forget every scrap of common sense she had left.

She stayed firmly where she was…

# CHAPTER FIVE

THEY HUNG A few more pictures, but this time he held them and she made the pencil mark, on the grounds that he was, as he put it, less likely to lose his grip.

She didn't argue. Frankly, ducking under his arm and being that close was complicated enough, especially when they were standing on his bed hanging the picture right over it.

The one that had hung over his bed before, the one that brought back memories that did nothing for her already compromised peace of mind.

'How's that?'

'Perfect.' If you wanted to be tortured…

She made the mark, he banged the nail in, hung it and stood back.

'Good. Right, that'll do. I've got my interview tomorrow and I need to check my suit and iron a shirt.'

She stifled a sigh of relief and walked out of the room. 'I'll head home,' she said quickly, wanting to get away before he said or did anything that might undermine her resolve, because the bed was much too close and far too inviting and she had a feeling they were standing on the edge of a precipice.

'Fizz first,' he said, heading for the kitchen. 'Well, unless you're driving?'

'No, I walked,' she said, unable to lie about it because he'd realise as soon as she opened the front door that there wasn't a car there apart from his.

She heard the soft pop of the cork, the fizzing of the glasses being filled, and he handed her one.

'Here.'

'Thank you.' She took it, vowing to go the moment it was finished, and clinked it gently on his. 'Here's to your new house—well, for now, at least. Maybe here's to a proper roof over your head and your own things around you.'

'I'll drink to that.' He smiled and clinked back. 'And here's to you, for all you've done to help me in the last few weeks, not least with the dog.'

'Where is she, by the way?' she asked,

picking up a scuffing sound. They found her in the pantry, chasing a paper plate around the floor with her tongue. The paper plate that had held the cake.

'Tatty!' he yelled, and she scooted out of the pantry looking guilty and a teeny bit smug.

'Oh, Ryan, that's my fault, I left it on the side! Will it hurt her?'

He shook his head. 'No. It wasn't a fruit cake or a chocolate cake. Lemon drizzle should be fine—well, fine for her, not so fine for me.' He sighed. 'I was looking forward to the rest of that.'

'When did you feed her? Because you haven't done it since I got here, I don't think.'

A look of guilty horror crossed his face, and he smacked his forehead with his palm. 'Lunchtime! Tatty, come here, sweetheart. I'm sorry. Are you a hungry girl?'

'That's so not your dog,' she said drily, and drained her glass, but she was trying not to laugh and the wine dribbled round the side of her mouth and down her front, and he put the bowl on the floor and walked back to her with a tissue in his hand.

'That'll teach you to laugh at me,' he said, his lips twitching, and he blotted her gently dry, lingering a little too long on the corner of her mouth.

She put the glass down, and he lowered the tissue and stared down into her eyes, his lips parting slightly, his eyes searching hers and finding—what?

She looked away hastily, slipping out from between him and the worktop and heading for the door while she still could.

'It's time I went home,' she said, her voice all over the place, and he followed her to the door.

'I'll bring Tatty and come with you, she could do with a little walk before bed,' he said, trashing her escape plan. It only took five minutes to walk her home, maybe a little more with Tatty sniffing every blade of grass to check it out, but then they were there, and she slid her key into the lock and turned back to him.

'Before you ask, I won't come in,' he said, and she nodded, trying not to look relieved because the air between them was still humming with whatever it was.

'Good luck tomorrow. I hope your interview goes well.'

He held her eyes. 'Are you sure you want me to go for it?'

Was she? She nodded, hoping he hadn't noticed her hesitation, because it wasn't really hesitation, she was just checking up on herself, making sure she could do this because after the sizzling tension between them this evening she really *wasn't* sure, because she had no idea where it was taking them.

Although it wasn't all about her, and they desperately needed another consultant…

'Yes, I'm sure. Thanks for seeing me home, Ry.'

'You're welcome,' he said softly, and cradled her face in his warm, gentle hands. 'Thank you again. For everything. I'll see you tomorrow.'

His lips brushed hers, just the lightest touch that lingered a moment, but fire scorched through her and she was ready to reach for him when he dropped his hands and turned away, and she let herself inside and closed the door, her legs suddenly like rubber.

Her fingers found her lips, pressing gently where his had touched hers, and she wanted to cry because his kiss had been so sweet, so tender, so unlike the raging passion they'd felt before two and a half years ago, or the kiss on the night he'd found Tatty, two weeks ago. So unlike the feelings she'd had when his hand had brushed her breast earlier today.

It had hardly been a kiss at all, and yet, as fleeting as it had been, she could still feel the rivers of fire flickering through her veins and reaching every part of her, and she'd been so close to inviting him in.

Thank goodness for Tatty, because he couldn't have stayed anyway and it might have been embarrassing.

She watched him walking away down the road in the dusk, Tatty at his side looking up at him devotedly, and she found herself smiling. Crazy man. He was deluding himself if he thought he'd rehome her.

She waited until they were out of sight, then turned and looked at the little silver heart sitting on its shelf. The heart that bound them together, no matter what else the future held, no matter where life took them.

She picked it up, cradling it in her hand, the dog forgotten.

'Your daddy's got an interview tomorrow,' she told Grace softly. 'He might be going to live near us permanently. I wonder how that will feel?'

She had no idea. No idea at all, of how

she'd feel or what the implications might be, and she felt horribly unsettled and confused.

Shaking her head, she pressed a goodnight kiss to the little heart, picked up a glass of water from the kitchen and headed upstairs for an early night, but sleep was a long time coming and she woke to the lingering fragments of a weird, disturbing dream that didn't make any sense but left her feeling even more unsettled.

She looked at the clock. It was only ten to six, and she was on a late so technically she could be having a lie-in, but she was wide awake after her run of nights and she felt suddenly unaccountably nervous for Ryan.

And for herself?

Because of course what happened today had massive implications for her, as well as him.

Would he get the job?

Did she even really want him to?

Yes—but what if he didn't get it? What if the other candidate was better after all? Or if there was another one who'd applied out of nowhere?

He'd leave if he didn't get it, but would that be the end for them? Probably. Let's face it, he'd made no attempt to keep in touch while he was with the aid organisation, so why would now be any different?

He had said he'd tried to phone her, and as she'd changed her number she couldn't blame him for that, although if he'd really wanted to he could have found her. Only he said he'd tried to airbrush her out of his life because he'd found it all too hard to deal with, so why would he have tried? And if he didn't get the job, he might well go back to MFA and do a better job with the airbrushing this time.

But if he got the job, then what? What would it mean for them as a couple? If they even were a couple...

They certainly weren't at the moment, and they'd never talked about that, never considered it, never mentioned the future. Was the future even in his mind, or was he simply looking for a job, loved the town and was happy to have her there as a friend?

Ugh. That word again, which covered everything from a slight acquaintance to—them? Maybe, as things stood. But would that be enough for her? She had a horrible feeling after yesterday that it wouldn't be, but on the other hand she wasn't sure what else there might be on offer apart from an affair, and she knew she didn't want that, or at least not in isolation, because her heart simply couldn't remain that detached.

It would need to be more than that, but how much more?

They hadn't lived together before, but maybe he would want them to this time, and where would that lead? If they fell in love, then maybe to marriage?

*A family?*

Her heart thumped against her ribs. Would he ask that of her? He'd said over and over again that he didn't want children, and he and Katie had split up because she'd tried to get pregnant without discussing it with him when she knew he was going away with MFA, possibly for several years.

But what if he'd changed his mind? What if it was only that he hadn't wanted to be an absent father? He'd said it was time for him to settle down now, to go back to the future. Did he mean with her, and if so, did he mean as a family, and if so, could she do it?

Only if he loved her, but she had no idea whether he did or not, except as a friend. She already knew she loved him, but enough for that?

Did she even dare to consider another pregnancy? Her body yearned for a child, her arms ached to cradle a baby, but she was so scared. Would she be brave enough to try again?

Her heart thumped, even the thought making her mouth go dry.

*Don't go there. It's all theoretical—and anyway, it might never happen. He probably isn't even thinking about it.*

And even if he was, there were so many unknowns. His interview, the job, their future together—only time would tell how their relationship would pan out, but she'd never been patient.

*One step at a time. Get the interview over, see if he gets a job offer, go from there.*

She threw back the covers, pulled on her clothes and went downstairs, made a cup of tea and took it outside, perching on the edge of the damp bench and staring at the garden in dismay.

It was ages since she'd done anything out here; she'd been so busy helping Ryan with Tatty or the house or both, and in that time spring had definitely sprung. Oh, well. She had all morning, and as soon as it was a civilised hour she'd cut the lawn, but until then she could do some weeding and tidy up around the edges and refill the bird feeders.

Anything rather than sit there with her nerves strung so tight she thought they'd snap...

'How did it go?'

Ryan gave a soft huff of laughter and tugged off his tie before it strangled him. 'I have no idea, Beth. OK, I suppose. I answered all the questions, but it was pretty tough. James didn't cut me any slack, but that was fine, I didn't expect him to, and he wasn't alone. The others were just as thorough.'

'What kind of questions?'

'Oh, I don't know, medical stuff and personnel management, mentoring, being a team player, that kind of thing, but also loads of ethical scenarios. What do you do if someone comes in in a coma and the person with them isn't down as their next of kin but is obviously very involved with them? The rights of children, the absence of a DNAR statement and the relatives saying don't resuscitate, they don't want it—all the usual stuff which gets handed up the food chain to the most senior person in the department at the time. How do you deal with staff members who've broken the rules? Do you cover your ass or do the right thing kind of questions.'

She bit her lip and he could see laughter sparkling in her eyes. 'I'm guessing you're not a cover your ass kind of person,' she said drily.

He chuckled. 'No. I'm not. So it might have lost me the job because I'd bet my life the other guy is.'

'Did you meet him?'

'Yes, but he had to leave suddenly. Cited family reasons, apparently, so they've postponed his interview for a week and he's coming back then.'

'So what was he like?'

He laughed again, wondering how to phrase it. 'Let's just say he seemed pretty confident.'

'Arrogant, then.'

He felt his lips twitch, and Beth chuckled. 'Oh, dear. That won't have gone down well with James. He's got no time for arrogance.'

'Ah, but, if he's good, if he comes over better than me in the interview—he's got a lot of experience, Beth, he's been a consultant for several years, and I'm pretty sure he thought they were only interviewing me because I was on site and they didn't have to pay travel expenses. He asked me where I'd been working, so I told him, and he then implied I'd been out of it for a while, which in a way I have, but not in a trauma sense. I'm sure I've covered far more in the last two years than he has. I don't think he had the slightest idea of how much I had to deal with. One minute you're fighting to contain an outbreak of Ebola, the next minute you're in a war zone and being shot at, then it's an earthquake and you're dragging people out of rubble during the aftershocks—it's crazy, and you pack more into every day than you ever would working here, busy though it is. And he wouldn't have lasted ten seconds, I don't think. I could be wrong.'

'I doubt it. It takes a special kind of person, I would imagine. I don't know how *you* did it.'

He huffed softly, seeing things he'd rather forget. Things that haunted his sleep. 'I didn't, always. I lost it a few times. Kids, mostly. That's what gets to you. The kids. You never forget their faces.'

'You never talk about it.'

'No. No, I don't.'

'More airbrushing?' she asked quietly, and he tried to smile.

'Probably.' He dragged in a breath and put the memories away. 'So, anyway, I've got to wait at least another week before I have the answer, so it's back to the day job for now. Want to fill me in?'

Her eyes were gentle, as if she could see what he could see, but her voice was quiet and steady and matter-of-fact, and he was grateful for that.

'The usual mayhem, I gather, not made better by you and James being out all morning, I don't suppose. I don't really know, I haven't been here long, I'm on a late today. I walked Tatty before I came in, by the way, and because one of Annie's boys isn't feeling well, I took Molly, too.'

'Oh, thanks. I was worrying about that. Amongst other things.'

'I thought you might be. I told Reg I'd walked her and fed her, but he's going to pop in a bit later anyway. I think he's enjoying it. Breaks up the day for him. I think he's been lonely since his wife died last year.'

He felt a pang of guilt for not knowing that. 'I didn't realise it was so recent, but I expect you're right, he will be lonely. What are you doing later?'

'What, like nine o'clock tonight later?' she said with a laugh. 'Nothing.'

'Good. Come round and I'll cook you dinner and we can celebrate me surviving my interview if nothing else. So what should I do now? Where do they need me?'

'I don't know. Sam's back, he's in Resus and he could probably do with a hand, he's only got Livvy and they're busy.'

'OK. I'll go and change. Tell them I'm on my way.'

She didn't get to his house until well after nine, and she couldn't get an answer, which was odd.

His car was there, but it was getting dark and she was pretty sure he wouldn't still be out with Tatty, so she let herself in and called his name, but he didn't answer and there was no sign of the dog and no lights on. Maybe they were still out?

She could smell something delicious cooking, though, so she went and investigated and found a fragrant casserole bubbling away a little too fast. She turned it down, stirred it and put the lid back on, and then realised the dining room doors were open to the garden, so she went out, her footsteps all but silent.

He was sitting on the steps, his elbows on his knees, his head hanging, and she knew instantly that something was wrong.

'Ryan?'

He looked up, and even in the dusk she could see he looked upset, and her heart stalled.

'Ry, what is it? What's happened? Where's Tatty?'

'Gone,' he said, his voice uneven, and she felt sick. 'The rescue centre rang. They had space in a foster home. I've just handed her over. The carer's going to keep her until she's had the pups, and then they'll rehome them all. They said they'd easily find her a new family, she's got such a lovely nature—'

His voice cracked, and she went over to him, sat down beside him and put her arms round him. 'Oh, Ry, I'm so sorry. I know how much you loved her.'

'I didn't love her,' he said angrily, his body stiff and resistant. 'She was a liability, and the last thing I needed! I'm well rid of her.'

'If you say so.'

'I do—and I don't want to talk about it.' He straightened up and shrugged out of her arms. 'I cooked a tagine.'

'I saw. I turned it down, it was starting to catch on the bottom of the pan.'

He groaned and met her eyes for the first time. 'Is it all right?'

'I think so. It's certainly cooked. It smells lovely.'

'Good. Let's go and eat it.'

He got to his feet and headed inside, but it was only when they got into the house she realised his eyes were red rimmed.

*Poor Ry. Such a kind heart, and so much love to give...*

'Can I do anything?'

He shook his head. 'No. I've just got to make some couscous. There's some of that fizz left. I recorked it—I found a gadget in my kitchen stuff. You could pour us some.'

'I've got the car here.'

'You can have one glass. Or you could stay.'

Their eyes clashed and held, and she looked away, her heart pounding. Stay, as in stay with him? Sleep with him? Make love, like they had before? What, to distract him from losing Tatty? She'd need a better reason than that.

'I don't think that's a good idea,' she said,

her voice a little uneven, and he laughed, a sad, bitter, broken laugh that wrenched her heart.

'No, you're right. Pour the wine, Beth. I can always walk you home again.'

She only had one glass, so he didn't need to walk her home, in the end, and he was glad he didn't, because it was only last night he'd done it with Tatty, and it would have felt weird without her.

Weird and wrong and sad—

Stupid. She was just a dog, for heaven's sake!

But all night, in the huge bed with more room than he could ever need just for himself, he worried about her, about how she'd be coping in unfamiliar surroundings, if the people would let her sleep on the bed with them or if she'd be banished to a shed—

No. Surely not a shed. He was being ridiculous. He rolled over, thumped the pillow and shut his eyes firmly, but he slept only fitfully for the rest of the night, and the following morning he was in work by seven.

So was Beth, and she gave him a searching look.

'Are you OK?'

'Of course I'm OK,' he said brusquely. 'Why wouldn't I be?'

She arched a brow and stood her ground. 'Have you had a coffee yet?'

'I've had about four. Why?'

She shrugged and propped herself against the wall. 'I thought a coffee might improve your temper. Obviously not.'

He sighed heavily and rammed a hand through his hair. 'Sorry. I'm being an idiot. I know she'll be fine.'

'She will. Really, Ry. She loves everyone—and everyone loves her.'

*Including him?*

Her hand on his arm was warm and comforting, but he shrugged it off. He didn't want to be comforted, he wanted to be left alone. 'So, what can I do for you, Beth?'

That eyebrow again. 'There's a patient due in Resus in a few minutes. You might be needed, so if you're not up for it, go and occupy yourself in Minors and I'll make an excuse for you.'

'I'm fine.'

She looked over his shoulder, and shrugged away from the wall. 'Good, because we're on. Are you coming?'

* * *

It was another busy week, but that was fine. He didn't want thinking time, not about anything and most particularly not about the dog, and events played into his hands, but then at three on Friday afternoon there was a sudden lull and everything stopped, so he took a break and headed off to the café, taking a coffee outside and sitting alone on a bench under a tree.

And there was a dog, a golden retriever who reminded him a little of Tatty, and he felt a lump in his throat.

What if she wasn't happy? What if she wouldn't settle?

He was being ridiculous. Of course she'd settle. All she needed was food and a sofa and she'd be fine.

*Wouldn't she?*

He pulled his phone out, hesitated, then rang the rescue centre and got put through to Zoe, the person he'd dealt with.

'Zoe, it's Ryan McKenna. I don't know if you remember me, I brought Tatty in to you on Tuesday.'

'Of course I remember you, Ryan. What can I do for you?' she asked, and he felt suddenly foolish.

'Probably nothing,' he admitted. 'I know you can't tell me anything, because she's not my dog and I hardly know her and I've handed her over to you so I've got no rights, but I'm just wondering if you can tell me how she is, if she's settled, you know—just to put my mind at rest?'

There was a sigh, and a few 'should I, shan't I' noises, and then she said, 'I can't lie to you. The person who's looking after her is worried. Tatty won't eat anything, she's hardly drinking, she's cried constantly and we're really concerned, but there's nothing you can do, I know that, and I'm sure she'll settle, given time.'

'But—what about her puppies? If she's not eating…'

'I know. And my foster lady's experienced, too. She's tried everything—even hand-feeding her boiled chicken, but she just takes a mouthful and then turns her head away.'

He felt the lump in his throat swell, and he swallowed and blinked hard.

'What if I had her back, just until after the puppies are born?' he said, wondering what he'd done with his brains but—how could he leave her there like that? Even if she was just a dog and it was really none of his business?

'Could you?' Zoe said, sounding doubtful. 'Would you be able to? What about your work commitments?'

'I can work round it. I've got a friend who helps me out—' assuming he hadn't upset her so much this week that she'd never speak to him again '—and my neighbour's been feeding her at lunchtime, so we can manage, I'm sure. I can't let her suffer. It's not fair. Not with the pups.'

There was a long silence, then Zoe sighed again. 'Can I call you back? I'll talk to the foster lady again, and my manager, see what they say, and I'll let you know.'

'OK. I'm at work so leave a message if you have to, I'll get back to you as soon as I'm free.'

He looked at his watch. Three eighteen. Another two hours and forty two minutes till he finished his shift. Assuming he finished on time, which was a big assumption. And then, maybe, he would be picking Tatty up.

Or not…

Time to get back. He swallowed his coffee, threw the cup in the bin and headed back to the ED, but the phone rang before he was even halfway there.

He glanced at the screen. Zoe. He answered, his heart in his mouth.

'What did she say?'

'No change. She thinks if you can manage it, she'd be relieved. She's even had the vet out because she was so worried about her puppies.'

He felt the air go out of him like a punctured balloon. 'OK. I'm still at work now but I can get her later. Just tell me when and where.'

Beth stared at him. 'You're doing *what*?'

'Picking her up at seven from the foster person. Beth, I have to. She hasn't eaten since Tuesday and she's crying constantly and they're worried. It's only till she has the pups.'

'Yeah, right. And you'll be able to give her up then?'

'Yes! Of course! This is just for the sake of the puppies and it's not for long,' he said, and she wondered who he was lying to, her or himself. 'The vet said she's probably due in two or three weeks. It's hard to say, apparently, and they can't tell how many puppies there are without an X-ray but she doesn't think it's a huge litter. Whatever, I can't let her suffer. Yes, it's a pain, but needs must.'

She eyed him sceptically. A pain? She didn't think so. Not for a moment. He looked relieved. And at least his horrible mood had lifted, because he'd been vile all week.

'Well, I'm glad to see you're happier. You might not be such a grump to work with now,' she said a little bluntly.

'Sorry.' His smile was rueful. 'I don't suppose you're around later, are you?'

'What, as a welcoming committee for the dog you don't intend to keep?' she teased, and the shutters came down again.

'Forget it. I just thought you might—'

'I'm sorry, I'm sorry. Yes, I'm around,' she said quickly. 'Of course I'm around. Do you want me to cook? I finish soon so I've got time. I can bring something over.'

'Could you? I've got to dive into the vets' to get some food for her on my way to pick her up, so I won't have time to shop, again! Are you OK with that?'

'Sure. I could do with picking up a few things.'

She detoured via the supermarket on the way home, made a chicken curry for them and poached some of the chicken in a little water for Tatty, because the dog's plight had pulled at her heartstrings and although she'd teased Ryan, she was fully behind his decision to have her back, whatever his motives.

Was it purely the dog? Or was it, in some subliminal way, to atone for his guilt for not being there for her after Grace? A determination not to let Tatty down the way he felt he'd let her down?

Whatever, she was sure both he and Tatty would be happier as a result, even if, inevitably, it would put some of the responsibility on her, but she didn't mind that and she'd been as worried as him all week.

He was back when she got to his house just after seven, and the dog ran to her for a quick cuddle before rushing back to her hero, and the look on his face said it all.

'I've made us a curry, and I cooked her some chicken,' she said, and he smiled at her properly for the first time in days.

'Thank you. I've got some dry puppy food from the vet for her. They said little and often, just till she's eating again normally. Why don't we mix it? Bit of each, just to tempt her?'

'I've made us lots of plain boiled rice, so she can have some of that, too.'

'Good idea.'

Tatty thought so, and while she ate, Beth dished up their curry and took it through to the dining room, and Ryan followed her, Tatty at his side, and sat down to eat nearly as hungrily as the dog, who was now lying on his feet. She wondered if he'd been eating, either. Maybe not. The man was riddled with guilt.

'She's clingy, isn't she? Even worse than before.'

He nodded. 'She is. Not surprising, really. At least she's eaten, though, so I can stop worrying about that. The curry was delicious, by the way. Thank you.'

'You're welcome.' She looked down at Tatty and smiled. 'Do you think she'd like it if we moved to the sofa?'

He laughed softly, but she thought she heard a tiny catch in his throat. 'I'm sure she would. Come on, Tatty.'

He got up, and she glued herself to his side and licked his hand continuously until he sat down, then jumped up beside him and settled with her head and shoulders on his lap.

His hand went down automatically to her side, and Beth saw him wince as he stroked her gently.

'She's so thin—she's back to square one. I'll give her more food in a while. They said little and often at first to give her stomach time to adjust, but she's just ravenous. Silly, silly girl, aren't you?'

'I can't believe she didn't eat all week.'

'Well, she certainly has now I've got her home.'

The word made her heart squeeze in her chest. Was it home? His, and the dog's? Did she even dare dream it might be theirs, down the line?

Yes, for now, but what if he didn't get the job? Although James had said something yesterday that she still hadn't had a chance to tell him.

She should, because until he knew about the job he was in limbo, putting one step in front of the other, day by day, with no idea where he was going. Well, at least not until he heard.

What if he didn't get it? Would he take Tatty with him wherever he went? And where would he go? He couldn't take her if he went back to MFA, although he'd said he wouldn't do that.

And what about her? What about them? Was there a 'them'?

She had no idea about that, either, but it was time she did, so she took a deep breath and tackled it head on.

'Ryan, we need to talk.'

# CHAPTER SIX

HE SWITCHED OFF the television he'd just put on and turned to look at her, searching her eyes for clues, but there were none.

'That sounds serious.'

'Not necessarily serious, but there's something I haven't had a chance to tell you. I don't know if it was significant, but I bumped into James yesterday as I was leaving work and he was asking me about you.'

'I thought he was on holiday?'

'He is, but he said he'd popped in for something. He wanted to know how I'd feel if they offered you the job.'

He felt his eyes widen. 'Are they going to? They haven't even interviewed the other guy yet, unless something's changed.'

'No, I think he was just sounding me out.'

'Why? I thought he didn't know about us? Unless you've told him?'

She shook her head. 'No, of course not. I haven't said anything to anyone, but he knows we know each other pretty well, and he may have put two and two together and come up with something which is obviously not even going to scratch the surface, but I wasn't about to put him right.'

'So what did you say?'

She looked away. 'I told him I'd be delighted for you if you got it, because I felt you deserved it, you're a brilliant doctor and would be an asset to the department, you love the town and I thought you'd be very happy here.'

He studied her carefully. 'Is that true?'

She looked confused for a second. 'Well—yes. Wouldn't you be happy here? And if not, then why *are* you here and why did you apply for the permanent post? And scrolling back, why did you apply for the locum job in the first place?'

'Because I needed a job. I told you that, and yes, I think I would be happy here. I *am* happy here. It's a lovely place, with a great hospital and the added bonus that you're here, so why wouldn't I be? That's not what I was asking, though. You said you'd be delighted if I got it, which rather implies you want me here.'

She looked confused again. 'I didn't say that. I said I'd be delighted *for you*. Not for me.'

'Or us?'

'Is there an "us"? Is there, Ry? I don't know. I don't even know if you want there to be an "us". Unless that's why you're here, after all.'

She cocked her head on one side and searched his face, her eyes suddenly filled with doubt. 'Are you *sure* you didn't know I was here?' she asked carefully, and he stared at her, slightly stunned.

'Absolutely. You know that. The fact that you're here was nothing to do with it because I didn't have a clue. I told you that weeks ago. I saw the locum job advertised, I needed something short-term until I worked out what I was doing with my life, and then you were here, but I had no idea you were, Beth. For heaven's sake, I'm not stalking you! Is that what you think?'

'No—no, of course not, but I'm still not sure why you applied for the permanent job—not really.'

He gave a little huff of laughter, feeling

lost in this circular conversation that didn't seem to be getting anywhere. 'Because it's a great place, and I love working here, and you said you were fine with it—are you not fine with it? Have you got a problem with it now?'

'I don't know,' she said, searching his eyes again, her own troubled. 'I honestly don't know, because I don't know where we stand, what we are to each other, where we go from here, if anywhere, because I don't even know you well enough to know if you're telling me the truth.'

He was shocked at that, a sick feeling in the pit of his stomach, and he stabbed his hand through his hair and stared at her.

'Why would I lie to you? It was sheer coincidence, I promise. I can't believe you'd think that of me. I'm not Rick!'

'I know you're not Rick. It's not that, it's nothing to do with him. He was a lying, cheating love rat and I know you're not that, but...'

'But?' he prompted, still smarting, and she shrugged.

'I just know we see things differently.'

'Such as?'

That little shrug again, touched with despair. 'I know you don't trust me, either. You don't trust anybody. When I told you I was pregnant...'

He let out a shuddering breath. 'Don't. I reacted badly. I know. I should never have accused you of getting pregnant on purpose. I know you're not like Katie, and you were hugely supportive of my decision to join MFA, but a bit of me wondered if you were just looking for an absent father, a convenient sperm donor. It's not unheard of.'

She looked stunned. 'Why would I want that? I'd just split up with Rick, I was bruised and battered emotionally, he'd been sleeping with my best friend and I'd lost them both— why would I suddenly decide to have a child on my own?'

'I don't know. You're right, we didn't know each other, we probably still don't, but I was wrong to jump to conclusions, and I'm sorry. And when I realised how serious things were with the pregnancy, I was gutted and I did what I could to help you, but it doesn't excuse how I was with you. But, no, you're right, I don't trust easily, any more than you do. I guess we're both wary, trying to protect ourselves, and sometimes that hurts other people.'

She nodded. 'Yes, it does. So—will you

do that again, if it gets tough? And what if I trust you, and let myself fall in love with you, and then we start having the difficult conversations?'

'Such as?'

She shrugged. 'I don't know—about starting a family, maybe—something I know you don't want to do.'

'I haven't said that.'

She stared at him blankly. 'You've said it over and over again!'

'To Katie, and about Katie and my relationship with her, because I was signing up with the aid organisation for the next few years and I had no intention of being an absent father! That doesn't mean I don't want children in the future. I'd love them.'

'With me?'

It was his turn to shrug, the question too close to home. 'Maybe, if that's the way this goes, but we don't know each other well enough yet to say that, Beth. We've shared a colossal history, in a way, and yet we're still strangers. We haven't reached a point in our relationship where we can see the future panning out, and that's one reason why I want this job, so we have time to see where it's going. If I don't get it and I have to move away, then we might find a long-distance relationship too much of a challenge, and I couldn't expect you to uproot yourself to come with me until we were both sure.'

'So you're just buying time?'

Was he? 'Maybe. I've made enough mistakes, hurt enough people, been hurt myself. I want to do it right this time, for you, for me, for us. And that means giving us time.'

'And you'll want children?'

He nodded. 'If it works between us, then yes, probably, I would, but not if you didn't feel you could do that. After Grace—I don't know. It must be hard.'

'It is. I do want children, desperately, but frankly I'm too scared to even consider it because I don't know if I can go through that again. And if I get pregnant by accident, would you blame me again? Say I've done it on purpose? What if I *can't* get pregnant again? What if we can never have a child? What if I'm just not brave enough?'

He stared at her, wondering how they'd got to this conversation when so far he'd hardly kissed her! Although it wasn't because he didn't want to.

He shook his head slowly. 'Why are we talking about this now?'

'Because I need to know how you feel so I don't end up letting myself fall in love with someone I know might break my heart! I can't be hurt like that again, Ry.'

'You said I hadn't ever hurt you.'

'You haven't—not yet. Well, maybe when you accused me of getting pregnant on purpose, but you didn't hurt me like Rick did, no. But this time, you might, because this time it's different. We're not starting from the same place. Before, we had total freedom and a lack of commitment, a relationship based purely on sex. It was all about fun, and it *was* fun, but we can't do that now, we can't go back to that and I wouldn't want to. Not after Grace. It would just feel wrong, as if we were trying to turn the clock back, but we can't. Grace died, and we can't change that, but I don't know how we move on from it. Who was it said you can't go back and make a new beginning?'

'C.S. Lewis,' he said quietly, his mind grappling with all the things she'd said. 'Well, it's been attributed to C.S. Lewis but that's been questioned. The actual quote is "You can't go back and change the beginning, but you can start where you are and change the ending". Maybe that's what we should be aiming for, because for us, where we left off, our ending was just heartbreaking, and maybe it's time to rewrite that, to make it the middle and not the end, and give ourselves a better ending.'

'Together?'

He shrugged. 'I don't know, Beth. That depends on so many things, some of which we have no control over. I just know we owe it to each other to leave ourselves in a better place than we were in. I don't want to hurt you, I never want to hurt you, but I don't know if I can give you what you want, what you need, and I don't know if you can give me that. I don't even know what it is I need and it doesn't sound like you do, either. All we can do is try. Try to understand, try to trust, try to care.'

'And if we fail?'

He searched her eyes, and tried to smile, but it was hard. 'Then at least we know we've done our best to heal each other,' he said quietly, and she closed her eyes and nodded.

'Yes.'

'So what do we do now, Beth?' he asked softly, and held his breath. What would she say? A light-hearted relationship, like they'd had before but without the disastrous consequences? No, she'd already ruled that out. A solid, straightforward friendship? Or something else, something deeper that would involve a greater commitment?

It felt like he'd tossed a coin and he'd only know what he wanted when it landed, but she shrugged again, a tiny shift of her shoulders, as if she didn't know what she wanted any more than he did.

'I don't know. I like you. I more than like you, much more, but—Ry, I don't know if I'm brave enough to test us. I don't know how strong we'd be together, how much we could lean on each other if life got tough. We couldn't before. Why would now be any better? If that was even what you wanted. I have no idea. You give nothing away—nothing at all, and I have no idea what you're thinking or feeling.'

'I can't tell you that, because I don't know,' he said after a long pause. 'I just know I want to see if we can make it work this time. We're not the same people we were. We've both changed.'

'But does that make us more compatible?'

'Not necessarily, but maybe more compassionate. I didn't stay with you when I should have done. I let you down, I know that. I wouldn't do it again.'

'But I didn't want you there, Ryan. I didn't want your pity, and I don't want it now.'

'No, I'm sure you don't. I wasn't offering it, then or now. But I don't know what you do want now, and if I'm honest I haven't got a clue what I want, either. Well, you. I want you, that hasn't changed, but I don't know if it's just physical still or if there's more than that, and if it's more I don't know how much more. Not now, not since Grace, because it's changed us both, tied us together in a way we'd never expected, and I don't know how we move forward from that. I just know that, one way or another, I'd like to have you in my life. I *need* to have you in my life, and if that means we have to test our relationship, to give it a try, then I'd like to do that to see if we've got what it takes, because I can't imagine living without you in my life in some form or other and I'm sick of living in limbo, too.'

'And what if we can't make it work?'

He shrugged. 'I don't know. Maybe we'd just have to try harder, because I can't imagine that I'll ever have a relationship with anyone else that comes near to being as profound and life-changing as what I've shared with you. And I don't know if losing Grace will be the thing that keeps us together, or drives us apart, but I just know it would be there in any other relationship I had with anyone else, and that getting past it would be unimaginably difficult. It'll be hard enough doing it with you.'

She nodded slowly, and a sad little smile flickered on her lips for a moment and then was gone.

'So what happens if you don't get the job?'

Her words hung in the air, and he felt the breath sucked out of him.

'I don't know, because it has all sorts of implications. But I certainly don't want to lose you.'

'And Tatty?'

'Tatty's going to be rehomed,' he said firmly, and hearing her name, she looked up at him and licked his hand.

'Yes, of course she is,' Beth said drily, and he swallowed hard and looked away.

'She is! Beth, if I don't get this job I won't have a choice, because I'll have to move on, I have no idea where, or how long for, so until I hear about it, I can't make any kind of commitment to her—or to you, come to that, because I'll have to get another job and it could take me anywhere. Anywhere at all.'

'I could maybe come with you. If you wanted me?'

That stunned him. He turned his head and met her eyes again. 'You'd do that?' he asked, slightly incredulous. 'You'd be prepared to uproot yourself again and follow me? What if it was somewhere you didn't want to go? And besides, it's only three weeks since you told me not to expect us to pick up where we left off.'

'I know. And I'm not sure how I'd feel about following you, but if our relationship was strong enough and the need arose, I should be prepared to. I guess there's only one way to find out. We need to try and open up more, talk to each other about our feelings. We need to give ourselves a chance.'

She held out her hand, and he stared at it for a moment, then slowly lifted his and threaded his fingers through hers, palm to palm.

'I guess so.'

He pressed a gentle kiss to her fingers, then laid their hands down again on Tatty's back. She turned her head and licked them both, then got off the sofa, stretched and lay down at his feet.

'Come here,' he said softly, turning towards Beth and giving her hand a little tug, and she shifted towards him. He slid his arm around her, tilting her face up to his with the tip of his finger, and then his mouth found hers in a kiss that lingered endlessly.

It would be so easy to take it all the way, to scoop her up and carry her into the bedroom, but they weren't ready for that yet, not emotionally, at any rate, and he didn't want to hurt her, so he eased away, turned the TV on again and settled back, Beth's head on his shoulder and the dog at his feet.

He could get so used to that...

'I should go home,' she said a while later.

Ryan met her eyes, and nodded slowly.

'Yes, you probably should. We don't want to rush this.'

'No. And it's not as if we don't know that the sex works,' she said with a wry smile, and instantly regretted it because she saw the heat flare in his eyes.

'Now why did you say that?' he murmured, lifting a lock of her hair back from her face, his fingertips skating lightly over her skin and making her shiver with need.

It would be so easy to reach up and kiss him, but it would never end with a kiss, so she pulled away and got to her feet and headed for the front door, and he followed, Tatty in tow as if she didn't trust him out of her sight. When they reached the door he drew her into his arms and hugged her gently, and she wrapped her arms around him and absorbed his warmth, wishing she could stay, wishing it wasn't such a bad idea.

Wondering where life would take them now.

'Drive carefully,' he murmured.

'It's just round the corner!'

'Yeah.' She could hear the smile in his voice. 'I know that, but it's Friday night and there are idiots about.'

She felt his fingers tunnel through her hair, and then he tilted her head and touched his lips to hers, warm and firm and so, so good. They clung, motionless, and then he groaned and deepened the kiss, nipping, biting, licking, parting her lips and delving until she whimpered.

He backed her against the wall, his knee nudging between her legs, rocking against her as he plundered her mouth. One hand was anchored in her hair, the other sliding under her top, his fingers splaying over her breast, and she arched into him, her body on fire, her hands on his back urging him closer.

'Ry...'

He swore softly and eased away, resting his forehead against hers as his breathing steadied, then he slid his hand round her back and pulled her close again and held her, his palm against her skin, cradling her head against his shoulder with his other hand so she could hear the echo of his heart thundering under her ear, his fingers toying with her hair for a moment before he straightened up and stared down into her eyes.

'Go home, Beth,' he murmured raggedly. 'We don't want to do something we could both regret.'

She nodded, went up on tiptoe and kissed his cheek, the stubble making her lips tingle all over again, and then with a pat for Tatty she opened the door and let herself out on legs that didn't quite work.

'Call me when you're home,' he said.

'What, so we can prolong the agony with phone sex?' she threw over her shoulder, and his eyes flared again, simmering with frustration.

'Just—call me,' he said through gritted teeth, so she did, the moment she got home.

'I'm safe. I survived the drunks and the idiots on the road. Are you happy?'

'No. Obviously I'm happy you're safe home, but if I'm honest I'd be happier if you were here finishing what we started.'

She swallowed, the teasing long gone, replaced by a deep ache overlaid by common sense. 'I would be, too, but if we're in this for the long haul there has to be more to our relationship.'

'I know. I still want you, though. That bed's awfully big.'

'I'm not sure Tatty would like sharing it.'

She heard him laugh and say something to the dog, then he was back. 'I need to feed her. She's hungry again, then I need to take her out for a little walk. Do you have any plans for tomorrow?'

'What, apart from working? I'm on a late.'

'Breakfast at the pub, and a dog walk?'

She smiled. 'Sounds good. Can we make it nine and walk her first? I start at twelve and I've got a twelve-hour shift, so a nice big breakfast at ten thirty would be good.'

'Sure. We'll walk round and pick you up. At least in daylight we're likely to behave ourselves. OK, Tatty, I'm coming. Sleep well, Beth. I'll see you tomorrow.'

'You, too.'

Sleep well?

In his dreams.

He had Tatty crushed up against him, as if she was making certain he was still there, and every time he moved she shifted back up against him again until he was clinging to the edge.

He didn't care. She was back, and anyway, he had plenty to think about while she kept him awake, starting and ending with Beth.

Did he love her? It certainly felt like love, or what he imagined it felt like. Not the white-hot physical craziness they had before, although that was still certainly there, but something much deeper and more profound, born of what they'd been through together.

Except they hadn't really been together, they'd just both been there, trapped on the same rollercoaster. The togetherness had been sadly lacking, but they'd been too wrapped up in shock and grief to forge a closer bond, and then he'd gone, leaving her to deal with it alone.

Could they make it work this time? Forge that bond now, two years later?

He hoped so. He knew he'd bust every sinew to give it a chance, but it wasn't just him, and she'd had more to deal with than he had.

Well, with Grace, anyway. He'd had all the MFA stuff, and some of the things he'd seen were pretty damaging. He wasn't quite unscathed, he knew that. The nightmares were a constant reminder, as were the scars, but it had to be worse for Beth.

He thought about her, about all the little ways she'd shown him kindness since he'd arrived in Yoxburgh. Would she have done that if she didn't care? He doubted it. Certainly no one else would, unless they were a better person than him—but then she was, he knew that.

There was no way she'd have left him the way he'd left her—except she'd told him she didn't need him and all but sent him away. Had she really meant it, or just said it to free him of his obligations? Probably.

Whatever, he'd gone, without a backward glance.

Well, he was back now, and it seemed they might have another chance, but only time would tell if it would work, and as for them having children—no, that was too far down the line to think about.

He rolled to his side, shoving Tatty out of the way, and finally he drifted off to sleep, only to wake from one of the many recurring nightmares to find the dog standing over him whining and licking his face.

He struggled up and propped himself against the headboard, turning on the light, and she lay on him, still washing any part of him that she could reach, as if to comfort him.

'It's OK, Tatty. I'm all right,' he murmured, and she rested her head down on his chest and watched him with soulful eyes.

He glanced at the clock. Four thirty. Too early to get up, and probably too late to go back to sleep again properly, but he ought to try.

He heaved her out of the way, turned off the light and lay down again, and she flumped back against him with a grunt.

'You're going to have to learn to share me,' he warned her, but he wasn't sure how that would work. Ah, well, Tatty would be gone soon, and until then maybe they'd find a way…

They had a lovely morning.

The weather was glorious, a beautiful spring day with everything bursting into life, and for a change they wandered through the little housing development she lived on, taking the footpath that cut behind all the gardens, with the cherry trees in bloom sprinkling them with confetti and the last of the daffodils and crocuses bobbing their heads in the grass verges. They crossed to the cliff top, following it to the steps and coming back along the beach, and Tatty was tugging at the lead.

'You could let her off.'

He raised an eyebrow and snorted, but then shrugged and took off the lead, and Tatty rushed into the sea, leapt back out and shook all over them.

'Got any more good ideas?' he asked, swiping water off his face with his hand, but she was too busy laughing at him to answer.

'Sorry.'

'I should think so,' he muttered, but he must have forgiven her because he took her hand in his and they strolled along the sand, with Tatty playing at the edge of the water.

He put her back on the lead when she soaked him again, but she'd got the tickles out of her toes and she trotted along peacefully beside them all the way to the pub.

They ate breakfast outside with her lying at their feet, smoked salmon eggs Benedict with wilted spinach and lashings of Hollandaise, washed down with copious coffee and followed up with a pastry just because why not, then she looked at her watch and sighed.

Was that really the time?

'I have to go. I've got a twelve-hour shift ahead of me, but at least I'm off then till Monday.'

'Lucky you. I'm on call from eight tomorrow morning until midnight, and then I'm working Monday, too. It's going to be gorgeous, I can hardly wait.'

She frowned at him. 'What about Tatty?'

He stared at the dog, lying asleep at his feet, and swore. 'Good point. She wasn't here when I said I could do it so it wasn't an issue, so I haven't even thought about it. If it's really busy, I might not get home. Damn.'

She waited, knowing what was coming, more than ready for it, and she heard him sigh.

'Yes,' she said, and he looked up and met her eyes.

'Yes?'

'Yes, I'll look after Tatty, and I can stay over tomorrow night if necessary—in the spare room,' she added, just so he knew. 'Then you can come and go if you have to, without worrying about her.'

He hesitated for an age, then nodded slowly. 'If you're sure…?'

'I'm sure. Are you done? I need to go. Duty calls.'

It was odd in the house without him the next day.

She spent a while with Tatty in the morning, then took her back to her own house and introduced her to it, picked up a few overnight things and the book she'd been trying to read for weeks, and walked back, her rucksack slung over her shoulder. And of course she met Reg on the drive, beaming at her through the gap in the hedge.

'Morning, Reg,' she said with a smile, and he gave her a nod.

'Morning. I see she's back, then.'

Tatty strained to get to him, and he eased through the hedge and gave her a little scratch on her head. 'Didn't think I'd see her again. I thought he'd sent her to the dog rescue?'

'He did, but she wasn't eating, so he went and picked her up on Friday. It's just until she has the puppies—or so he says, but he's a bit of a softy.'

'I can see that, just how he is with her. I was surprised when he said he'd taken her. I didn't think he would.'

'No, nor did I, but whatever, she's back for now, and I'm dog-sitting until tomorrow because he's at work.'

He tilted his head on one side. 'I can look after her, if you like? You know, while the two of you are at work. She's good company. I don't mind at all, any time.'

He looked so hopeful, so desperately lonely, and she knew how that felt, from the yawning void after Grace had died when nobody knew what to say to her so said nothing or just plain avoided her.

'You'll have to talk to him, but I'm sure he won't say no. He's very grateful for your help.' She hesitated, then stifled her selfish urge to curl up with a book and went on, 'Reg, what are you doing this afternoon? It's just that Ryan's garden is a bit of a mess, and I thought I might have a go at it but I'm not sure what's what, really, and your garden's immaculate, so I thought you might be able to give me some pointers.'

All of which was a lie, because she hadn't had any intention of working in the garden, Ryan had already done quite a lot of tidying, and she knew exactly what was what down to the last perennial poking its head out of the earth. But the old man's eyes lit up, and he nodded.

'I'll just get myself a bit of lunch, and I'll be over. Leave the gate unlocked, I'll come round the side.'

That was odd. He could hear laughter coming from the garden, Beth's and someone else's. He let himself in and walked through the house, to find her sitting on the garden steps, Reg beside her with a mug in his hand and Tatty lying on the floor at their feet, dismantling a supposedly indestructible dog toy.

'Hi, all,' he said, and Tatty thumped her tail as he crouched down and gave her a tickle.

Beth smiled at him. 'Hi. Good day?'

'So-so. It won't last. What have you three been up to?'

'We've been gardening. Reg kindly offered to lend me a hand and show me which were the weeds and which weren't,' she said, staring pointedly at him, and he stifled the smile.

'That's kind. Thanks, Reg. Horticulture's not my strong point and I'm not sure it's Beth's, either.'

'Ah, well, she asked the right person, then. I was a nurseryman for fifty years. Only gave up when Queenie got sick, so if there's anything you need to know, you only have to ask.'

'Thank you. That's very kind. I'll bear it in mind.'

Reg gave the dog a pat and got stiffly to his feet. 'Well, I'd better be going then,' he said.

'You're welcome to stay,' he heard Beth say. 'I was going to make a salad, there's plenty.'

'Ah, now, that's very kind, my dear, but salad doesn't agree with me, and I've got a nice piece of fish from the hut down by the harbour, freshly caught this morning. I'll make a bit of batter later and pop it in my fryer. Won't be as good as my Queenie's, but it'll do. I might have a nap first.'

He gave Tatty a little pat, then Ryan showed him out, thanked him again and went back to Beth.

'Show you what's a weed and what's not? Really?' he murmured, and she smiled, but her eyes were filled with sadness.

'Yeah, I know, but he was so lonely, Ry. He loves looking after Tatty, he says she's good company. I think he might be spending most of the day here, you know, while you're at work. It must be so lonely for him without Queenie. They were married for sixty-five years, and she only died last July. She had Alzheimer's and she didn't know him any more, but he kept her at home right to the end, and I think he's just lost now. It's so sad.'

Poor Reg. Trust Beth to get him to open up. It was her all over.

'You're a good person, do you know that?' he murmured softly.

'I just felt so sorry for him. That awful empty ache…'

An ache she must know only too well.

'Oh, Beth.'

He pulled her into his arms and hugged her, resting his cheek against her hair and breathing her in, fresh air and sunshine and Beth, and it felt so good coming home to her.

Fingers crossed their fledgling relationship might stand a chance of flourishing into something that could stand the test of time, like Reg and Queenie's had.

He could only hope.

'Right, I haven't got long but it was quiet so I thought I'd make a break for it for a while, so can we eat? I haven't had anything apart from a biscuit since this morning.'

'Sure, it won't take a minute.'

She went up on tiptoe and kissed him, and it would have been so easy to take it further, but he was still on call and he didn't want to start something he might not be able to finish, so he eased away, hugged her again and led her back into the house.

# CHAPTER SEVEN

TATTY WAS FUSSING.

Beth had no idea why. She'd had a walk, been fed, been out in the garden again, and Beth wondered if she was going into labour.

No, surely it was too early? The vet had said another two to three weeks. But she'd kept running to the door and whining, and now she was barking, so Beth got up to let her out again, this time following her into the garden.

'What is it, Tatty?'

She couldn't see or smell anything, but then Tatty barked again, standing and facing Reg's bungalow. She went up the steps to get a better look, and to her horror saw flames in his kitchen.

*Dear God...*

'Oh, Reg... Tatty, come here.'

She called the dog back in, grabbed her

phone and keys, and ran out of the front of the house, through the hedge, banging on Reg's front door while she dialled 999.

No answer, and it was locked, of course.

*Back gate. Please be open...*

She ran round to the side, pushed the gate and it opened, and she gave the address to the emergency services, asked for fire and ambulance and tried the back door.

*Eureka.* She was in, and she shoved her phone in her pocket and turned off the gas ring. The pan was still burning but she knew better than to touch it, so she ran through into the hall, closing the door behind her to try and stop the smoke from spreading.

'Reg? Reg, where are you?' she asked, but the air was filled with smoke so she opened the front door wide and to her relief heard the sound of sirens.

'Reg! Reg, it's Beth. Where are you?'

A nap. He'd said he was going to have a nap, but not necessarily in bed.

*Be systematic.*

She started with the room beside the kitchen, but it was empty, so she went to the next, and there he was, sitting in his chair clutching his chest, his eyes wide with fear.

'Beth—the chip pan—can't breathe—'

'It's OK, Reg. The fire brigade are here now—see the flashing blue lights? And there's an ambulance, in case you need it. They'll take you to hospital to get checked over, but I need to get you out—'

'I can't leave—Queenie. She's on the mantelpiece. I can't leave her, Beth…'

'It's OK,' she promised. 'I won't leave her, Reg, but you need to get out now.'

He nodded, just as the fire officer ran in and assessed the situation at a glance.

'Fire's in the kitchen. I've turned the gas ring off but it's still burning,' she told him.

'That's all right, we're dealing with it, but you need to leave the house now.'

'We will. Reg, can you manage to walk to the ambulance?'

He nodded, but he was shaking like a leaf so the fire officer scooped him up in his arms and carried him into the front garden, and she scooped up Queenie and ran out after them.

'Queenie,' he coughed, but she shook her head.

'It's OK. I've got her here, Reg.'

'If I go, bury me with her—'

'You're going nowhere but the hospital,' she said firmly, 'and I'm going to follow you in my car, and ring Ryan and tell him to expect you. If you think for a moment he's going to let you die then you're underestimating him.'

She turned to the paramedics. 'Look after him. I've just got to put his wife's ashes next door and lock up and I'll follow you, but if you get there first, tell them to get Ryan McKenna.'

'Beth?'

He got to his feet, abandoning the notes he was writing up because her face had black smudges on it and something was clearly wrong.

'Are you OK? What's going on? What are you doing here?'

'I've come in with Reg. He had a chip pan fire in the kitchen.'

'Is he all right?' He sniffed. 'Beth, you stink of smoke. Tell me you didn't go in?'

'I had to. I wasn't going to leave him, Ryan. It hadn't spread so I turned off the gas and shut the door and found him—'

'You what? Beth—'

He swore, hauled her into his arms and hugged her hard, his heart hammering.

'What were you thinking? You should have called the fire brigade!'

'I did, and the ambulance, but I wasn't going to wait and watch his house go up in smoke. He was worried about Queenie. He wouldn't leave her ashes. I had to make him come here, and the only way I could get him out was to bring her, too, so her ashes are in your study. I hope that's OK.'

'Of course it's OK. So how is he?'

'Respiratory distress, maybe from smoke inhalation? I don't know, there wasn't that much, it could just be shock. He couldn't walk, but there wasn't really any smoke in the sitting room where he was. His breathing was awful, though, so I don't know how much of it was panic.'

'What kind of smoke was it?'

'Oh, it was only the oil, the kitchen hadn't caught fire, but it was pretty stinky. I think they put it out really fast, though.'

'Oh, well, that's all right then,' he said wryly, rolling his eyes. 'Although of course you didn't know that when you went in. Right, we'll get you both checked over.'

'I'm fine. I'm not stupid, Ryan, I didn't inhale it. You need to worry about Reg. I promised him you wouldn't let him die but his heart was misfiring a bit.'

He grunted. 'Great. Has he got atrial fibrillation?'

She shrugged. 'I don't know. Possibly. He had a triple bypass last year, apparently, but he was very shaken. It would be easy to say he's a tough old bird, but—he said if anything happened, bury him with Queenie, but I'd rather he didn't get to that point.'

Ryan nodded. 'Yeah, me, too. Have they got children? Anyone we need to contact?'

'I don't know. He didn't mention children, but I didn't get his entire life story this afternoon,' she said with a smile, and he wiped the smuts off her cheek and kissed her, frowning at the frizzled ends on a lock of her hair. Jeez...

'Let's hope we don't have to worry about it,' he murmured, letting it go for now, and they went to find Reg.

It was nearly eleven before she got home, leaving Reg safely tucked up in bed on a ward with a heart monitor just to be on the safe side and Ryan more or less happy that she wasn't about to die of smoke inhalation.

He'd given her another lecture, though,

about not waiting for the fire brigade before she went in, but she'd ignored it, knowing full well he'd have done exactly the same thing.

The fire engine was gone but the response car was still outside, to her surprise. Maybe it had been worse than she thought, but at least Reg's home hadn't burned to the ground. If she'd gone to bed, or ignored Tatty…

She went up the drive and knocked on the open door, and the firefighter who'd carried Reg out appeared. 'How is he?'

'He's OK. He's staying in overnight. I promised I'd come and get some stuff to take in to him, but I'll do that tomorrow. I'm surprised you're still here. Is the house OK?'

'Yes, it's fine. I was just filling in the paperwork before I leave, but the kitchen needs a deep clean to remove the smoke residue.'

'I'm sure we can sort that out. He was all for coming home tonight but I talked him out of it.'

'He was lucky you were here. Was it you who raised the alarm?'

She nodded. 'Yes—I was next door. The

dog started fussing, so I went out in the garden to find out why, and I saw the flames.'

The man eyed her thoughtfully. 'He's lucky you did. You saved his life, there was no way he was getting out and it would have gone up. And well done for not trying to put the fire out, although you could have had serious burns even just turning off the gas.'

She smiled a little wryly. 'Oh, I know. I'm a nurse in the ED. I've seen what can happen with a chip pan fire, and it isn't pretty, especially if they put water on it. I give the "call the fire brigade and get out" message over and over again, so I wasn't going to forget, and I was very careful.'

'Good, but don't do it again. Right, I'm ready to go, so if I could give you the keys?'

'Yes, of course. And thank you so much for all you've done.'

'All part of the job, my love. You know that as well as I do.'

He locked the door, handed her the keys and headed down the drive, and she went through the hedge and let herself in to a rapturous welcome from Tatty.

'It's all right, sweetheart,' she crooned. 'Come on, come and have something to eat, and then I need a shower because I stink.'

* * *

She'd just got out of the shower and wrapped herself in a towel when she heard a car, and Ryan appeared in the doorway behind her.

'Are you OK?'

Was she? Maybe, maybe not.

She felt herself well up, and walked into his arms, suddenly desperate for a hug.

'He wouldn't leave Queenie, Ry,' she said tearfully. 'He was going to stay there and die rather than leave her. If I hadn't been here, if Tatty hadn't warned me—'

'Don't.' His arms tightened around her, one hand cradling the back of her head and pressing it hard against his shoulder, the other firmly round her waist. 'He's OK, and so are you, but all I've been able to think about is what would have happened if anything had gone wrong. I could have lost you, Beth. You could have died, or been horribly burnt—'

His voice cracked, and she tilted her head and cradled his cheek in her hand.

'I'm fine, Ry. I'm OK. Nothing happened.'

'This time. But don't ever—ever—do that kind of thing again, OK?'

'You would have done it, too, you know you would. You've probably done far worse.'

'Yes, I have, but that's no excuse, and it wasn't a good idea. You were lucky, Beth. So lucky. Your hair's singed, for God's sake. You could have died. I could have lost you...'

His grip slackened, and he cupped her face in his hands, staring intently into her eyes, and then his mouth found hers in a desperate and yet tender kiss that turned her legs to jelly and her heart to mush.

She felt the towel fall away, dropping to the floor and leaving her naked in his arms, and he stared down at her, his eyes a little wild.

'I want you, Beth,' he grated. 'I need you. When I think about what could have happened...'

She nodded. 'I need you, too,' she said, her voice uneven. 'I didn't even think about it until afterwards, and then—'

She broke off, and he kissed her again, his whole body trembling, then he took a step back and stripped off his clothes and hauled her up against him as his lips found hers again, their legs meshing, the tension that had wound tighter and tighter finally snapping as their bodies came together.

There was no finesse, no foreplay, no tenderness, just a terrible urgency, a raging need to hold and be held, to be as close together as they could be until she couldn't tell where she ended and he began.

'Wait.'

He let go of her, yanked open the bathroom cabinet and pulled out a condom, his fingers shaking.

'Let me.'

'No. I'm too close.'

And then he was back, lifting her against the tiles and driving into her with a ragged groan. The spring coiled tighter inside her with every thrust, every touch, every heartbeat, and then she felt it shatter and she clung to him, sobbing his name as he slammed into her one last time.

He caught her cry in his mouth, his body stiffening, and then he slumped against her, chest heaving, his head on her shoulder, breath rasping in her ear, and then he lifted his head and stared down into her eyes.

'I'm sorry...'

'Don't be. I think we both needed that.'

He laughed softly and lowered her until her feet touched the floor, then eased away, turning to deal with the condom, and she frowned.

'Ry?'

She ran her hand lightly down his back, feeling the sweat-slicked skin, the strong columns of muscle, the—scars?

*It wasn't a good idea.*

Was that what he'd meant when she'd said he'd probably done far worse?

'What happened to you, Ry? What did you mean just now when you said it wasn't a good idea?'

He turned back to her, his mouth tipped into a smile, if you could call it that.

'There was a shell. I shouldn't have been where I was, but I was trying to get back into the hospital. It had been bombed, and my friends were in there trying to salvage what they could, and I wanted to get them out, to warn them that it wasn't safe, and there was another one.'

He looked away. 'I was the only one who made it out, and only just. As I said, not a good idea.'

'Are these the friends you said you'd lost? The ones whose death made you decide to stay and carry on their work?'

He nodded, his eyes meeting hers again. 'Yes. But I was careful after that—well, when they let me out of hospital. I was hit by shrapnel.'

'Shrapnel?' She looked down at his body, searching it for signs, but then he turned his back to her again and she saw the other scars, peppering his back and legs. She reached out and touched them. So many of them, some so small she could hardly see them, others bigger, as if the holes had been enlarged. Those were the ones she'd seen, the ones she'd felt.

'Did they get it all out?'

He turned back towards her, his mouth tilted into a wry smile. 'Mostly, but let's just say it wouldn't be a good idea to put me in an MRI scanner.'

She winced. 'Well, it would get all the last bits out, I suppose,' she said drily, and he chuckled and pulled her back into his arms.

'You have such a bad sense of humour,' he murmured, and kissed her again, tenderly this time, his hand stroking her damp, tangled hair. 'You need to deal with this or it's going to dry in knots, and I probably should go and talk to the whining dog. Have another shower, and I'll follow you.'

He kissed her again and let her go, and she stood in the shower and rewashed her hair, this time using the conditioner that she'd taken over there for Tatty, and she was almost done when she felt his hands on her, turning her into his arms as he stepped into the shower behind her.

'Are you OK? I was a bit rough, but I couldn't think about anything but getting close to you, so close I could feel your heartbeat so I knew you were still alive.'

'Don't you think you're being a bit dramatic?' she said softly, but he shook his head.

'No. If you'd seen what I've seen…'

'Tell me.'

'No. There are things you don't need to know, things I don't need to remember.'

He rested his head against hers. 'I still can't believe you went in there,' he said, his voice unsteady, and she hugged him hard, feeling the tension in his body.

'I'm fine, Ryan. I know it was stupid, looking back on it, but at the time it was no big deal and I'd probably do it again. I couldn't have let him burn to death, I couldn't have lived with myself.'

'No, I get that, I do. You just scared the spit out of me.'

'I'm sorry. How is he, by the way?'

'OK. He might have AF. They're monitoring him. How did you know he'd had a triple bypass?'

'I saw the scar when they were doing the ECG, and I asked him. He only had it done last year, after Queenie died. He wouldn't do it before. He's such a good man.'

'He is, and I'm glad you saved his life.' He let her go, stared down into her eyes and then bent his head and kissed her again, with a touch of desperation. 'Even so, don't ever do anything like that again, please,' he muttered gruffly against her mouth.

She stroked her fingers lightly over his cheek. 'I'm fine, Ry. You look shattered. You need to go to bed.'

'Come with me. I still need to hold you.'

'Tatty might have a view.'

'Tough. She can find herself somewhere else to sleep.'

'Unlikely. I'll come and join you both. You finish your shower and sort the dog out, and I'll dry my hair and see you in a minute.'

She was more than a minute, but not much, and he was lying in the middle of his bed, with Tatty beside him. She got in on his other side, and he pulled her into his arms, cradling her face against his shoulder.

'OK?'

She nodded and yawned. 'I feel exhausted. It's so late—what time is it?'

'Nearly one. Go to sleep, my love. I've got you.'

She tilted her head and kissed him fleetingly, then settled against him, comforted by his warmth and the strong, steady beat of his heart as she fell asleep in his arms.

He couldn't sleep. All he could think was that he could have lost her.

If the chip pan had exploded, or the gas line to the cooker, or any one of a dozen other things, he could have lost her.

It must have taken such courage to go in there. Courage and humanity, things Beth had in spades, it seemed.

She'd even rescued Queenie's ashes to put Reg's mind at rest.

God, he loved her. He hoped he'd get the job, so they could stay here and make this their home, start a new life together, but there was the other candidate to consider. He had his interview tomorrow—no, today. It was today.

He hoped he didn't run into him. He might be tempted to sabotage him.

Beth whimpered in her sleep, and Tatty

got up, walked over him and lay down beside her. He shifted slightly to give them both more room, and Beth snuggled closer in her sleep.

It felt so good to hold her. Really good…

He fell asleep with a smile on his face.


She woke to a kiss, and she opened her eyes and smiled up at him.

'Morning.'

'Mmm. It is, and I have to go to work, but first…'

He kissed her again, his touch tender this time, lingering and full of promise.

'Do you have to go?' she asked as he pulled away, and he gave a wry chuckle.

'Sadly I think I do, especially if I want the job. The other guy's got his interview today and shirking doesn't look good.'

She smiled at that. 'Probably not. Go on, then. I'll see you later. I start at twelve again, but just till nine so it's a bit more civilised. You can cook for me, if you like?'

'Or we could go out for dinner?'

She shook her head. 'No. Let's stay in. Reg won't be here so we need to spend time with Tatty. I'll take her for a quick walk soon, then again before I come in, but I've got to take some things in for Reg as well, so I might do that mid-morning. Want to grab a coffee then?'

'If there's time. Come and tell me how he is.'

'OK. I'll see you later.'

He kissed her again and left, and she spent a few more minutes coming to, listening to the sound of Tatty chasing her bowl around the kitchen floor, then she threw back the covers and went into the bathroom and caught sight of herself in the mirror.

Her hair was dishevelled, her eyes had smudges under them, but she was smiling, and she realised that for the first time in a very long while she felt happy.

Not just content, but genuinely, truly happy.

Humming under her breath, she washed and dressed, glad she'd brought clean clothes because the ones she'd had on yesterday really did smell awful, and then after she'd walked Tatty she let herself into Reg's house.

The smell was still lingering in the air, and she guessed it would take a while to shift. She found him some wash things in the bathroom, and had a hunt for some clothes because the ones he'd been wearing would smell of smoke, but the first cupboard she opened was full of women's clothes, like a giant memory box for Queenie.

She fingered the sleeve of a pretty blouse, and felt her eyes fill. Poor Reg...

*Core business.*

She opened the next cupboard and found what she was looking for, pulled out trousers, a shirt, some underwear and pyjamas, and left for the hospital.

He was sitting out in the chair when she arrived, and she perched on the bed beside him with a smile.

'You're up bright and early,' she said, and he nodded.

'I couldn't settle. I was worried about the house.'

'No need to worry, Reg. The house is fine. They were still there when I got back last night, but the kitchen isn't damaged, and it's all locked up, though it's a bit smelly, I'm afraid.'

He nodded. 'I thought as much. But the rest is all right?'

'Yes. It'll be fine, I'm sure. But how are you, that's the main thing?'

'Oh, I'm all right, Beth. Don't know why I'm here, really. I'd rather be at home.'

She took his hand and squeezed it. 'I'm sure they won't keep you in any longer than they think is necessary. We were a bit worried about your heart and your breathing.'

'Oh, I've always been a bit wheezy. I'm best outdoors, really. I always have the windows open, even in the winter. I guess that's how you smelt the fire.'

'The dog warned me. She was fussing.'

'Was she? Bless her. I was so pleased to see you last night, Beth. I thought I was going to die in there…'

His eyes filled, and he patted her hand with his other one, and she clasped it.

'But you didn't. Why didn't you go outside? Come round to me and raise the alarm? Was it because of Queenie?'

He nodded, and she felt her own eyes well.

'Oh, Reg. She's safe. She's in Ryan's study, waiting for you to come home. Do you have any family we can contact for you?'

He shook his head. 'No. We were never blessed with children, and all the rest of my family have died. That's what happens when you get old, girl.'

She nodded, then glanced at her watch and sighed. 'I'm sorry, I'm going to have to go, I've got to walk Tatty again and give her lunch and I start work at twelve, but I've brought you in some clothes. I have no idea if they're the right ones, but if not I can go back to get some others. And I've brought some wash things. I'll be back later to see you. I'll just go and tell Ryan how you are.'

She kissed his grizzled cheek and eased her hands away from his, and he let her go with obvious reluctance.

Ryan was just coming out of Resus when she got down there, and she caught him up with Reg's progress.

'His breathing's much better now. They might discharge him later today, but he hasn't got any family so goodness knows where he'll go.'

'We'll keep an eye on him, don't worry. As you said he spends most of his time with Tatty, and we're in and out. Got time for coffee?'

'Probably. What about you?'

'Probably not, but the other candidate's having a guided tour so to be honest I'd rather make myself scarce for a bit.'

'You don't want to show off?'

He snorted. 'I did have a childish urge, but it's quiet—'

'Adult trauma call, five minutes. Paediatric trauma call, five minutes.'

She laughed at the dirty look he gave the tannoy speaker. 'Here's your chance, McKenna. I'll leave you to it. Knock their socks off.'

His chuckle followed her as she walked away, and she couldn't stop the smile on her face.

# CHAPTER EIGHT

THE NEXT FEW days were hectic, but luckily Reg was back home by Monday evening, a little shaken still but seemingly unscathed, and when Ryan suggested that they could juggle their shifts so he didn't need to worry about helping out with the dog, Reg looked so crestfallen that he relented.

In return, though, he cleaned and repainted the old man's kitchen on his day off, and gave him a lecture on safety and an electric chip fryer that only used a teaspoon of oil, and they juggled the odd shift without telling him.

The upside was that Tatty was spending lots of time with Reg in the run-up to her puppies, which as far as they were concerned was a win-win, because it kept both the dog and the old man happy, and one or other of them would walk her before and after work.

And since she seemed to be spending most nights with Ryan, Beth moved some of her things there. First a toothbrush, then some underwear and a couple of tops, her trainers for dog walking, then some work clothes...

She wasn't there every night, but the nights she was—those nights were everything she'd remembered, and more.

She'd forgotten just how in tune their bodies were, how responsive she was to every touch, and their lovemaking now had an extra edge that it hadn't had before, an exquisite tenderness that left her feeling cherished. Because he loved her? Or at least she supposed he did, although he hadn't said it yet in so many words.

She wished he would, not least because it was on the tip of her tongue all the time, but she guessed he was holding back until he was certain how he felt. After all, it wasn't just her who'd been affected by Grace's death, and he'd had all the aid stuff to deal with. The fallout from that must have been pretty devastating at times, although he hadn't said a lot. Not that he ever did, but she was getting to know him now, and she knew there was no way he'd tell her anything until he was ready.

Then at the end of the week a woman and child were brought in from an RTC. The fire crew had cut them out of the car, and although the mother seemed uninjured, the child was struggling to breathe and she refused to leave him.

'Right, let's get the clothes off and have a look,' Ryan said, reaching for his stethoscope. 'We need CXR, echo and let's get him on one hundred per cent oxygen. Can you tell me what happened?' he asked the mother, and Beth looked at her and frowned.

She looked OK, and yet there was something...

'I—I swerved. There was a dog. I must have hit the kerb, and the car just rolled over and over. I wasn't even going fast. Don't make me go. I can't leave him.'

'It's OK, you don't have to,' Beth said softly, putting an arm round her. 'He's in good hands. Come and sit down over here and give Emma all your details, and let us do our job. We'll make sure you know what's going on.'

'Don't let him die—'

'Not my plan,' Ryan said, but his face was oddly expressionless and Beth's pulse hiked.

'Beth, I need you, please. I think we've got a tamponade.'

He was listening to the chest, looking at the little boy's neck, checking the monitor.

Low blood pressure, she noticed, but only slightly, and he was tachycardic. 'Are you sure?' she murmured, out of the mother's earshot.

'No, but I want an echo. Can I have the FAST scanner, please? And where's the radiographer?'

'I'm here,' Sue said, coming in, and moments later they had a picture of his chest on the screen, confirming the FAST scanner's findings.

'Increased cardiac silhouette, so he'll need pericardiocentesis,' Ryan said, and then the monitor began to bleep and he said something under his breath and met her eyes. 'Someone call cardiology, please, and, Beth, can you talk Mum through pericardiocentesis and then give me a hand, please? I'll get him prepped.'

Great. Tell a worried mother someone was going to stick a huge needle into the boy's chest and suck blood out from around his heart before it killed him. She sat down beside her and took her hand.

'Mrs Gray—'

'Louise, please. What's he doing to Tim?'

'It looks like he's got fluid around his heart, under the pericardium, the membrane that surrounds it, and that's pressing on the heart muscle and stopping it from doing its job, so what we need to do is put a needle in, very carefully, and draw off the fluid.'

'What kind of fluid?'

'Blood, most likely. It looks as if he might have a bleed in there, possibly from the collision.'

She shook her head. 'But there wasn't really a collision. I don't understand. Was it the seat belt? He's in a five-point harness—it can't be that.'

'There's an old bruise on his chest,' Ryan said, turning his head. 'Has he fallen recently, in the last week or so?'

'Um—yes, a couple of days ago. More, maybe. He fell downstairs and landed on a toy. He was only halfway up, but he was being silly. He's always silly, he's a boy—'

She pressed her hand over her mouth, and shook her head. 'He seemed fine, and then today he was tired and didn't seem to want to do anything. I was going to take him to the doctor if he wasn't better tomorrow, but it's the weekend. I should have gone today—'

'Well, you're here now,' Beth said, 'and maybe it wasn't that, but at least you're here and you're in the best place. I need to go and help, but Emma will stay with you.'

She nodded, her face contorted with fear for her son, and Beth went over to Ryan, who was already gowned and gloved.

'Cardiology can't spare anyone fast enough so I want you to help me,' he said quietly.

'What do you need?'

'A twenty-one-gauge spinal needle with the trocar removed, a five mil and thirty mil syringe, a three-way tap and T connector.'

'OK.'

By the time she was ready he was poised with the needle just under the bottom of Tim's sternum, aiming for his left shoulder and advancing the needle in little jerks, under the guidance of the FAST scanner wand she was holding, until the syringe suddenly began to fill with blood.

'OK, I'm in. Let's get the T connector and tap on it, and get this fluid off.'

He was still drawing off the fluid when the boy's respiration rate and heart rate slowed, his blood pressure picked up and his breathing steadied.

'Well done,' she said softly, and he looked up, his eyes suddenly bright.

'Yeah. I didn't want to lose this one.'

*This one?*

She straightened up and smiled at Louise across the room.

'He's looking better already,' she said, and Louise put her hand over her mouth and stifled a sob. Her other hand, Beth noticed, was lying against her abdomen, almost cradling it…

'Are you done with me?' she asked Ryan quietly. 'I've got a bad feeling about Louise.'

He glanced over his shoulder and nodded. 'You go. He's fine. We'll ship him up to PICU shortly, they can continue to monitor him but I think we've done enough for now.'

She went over to Louise and sat down again, taking her hand. 'Louise, I think I need to have a look at you. You might have been hurt by the seat belt.'

Her eyes flared wider, and she sucked in a breath. 'My baby,' she whispered. 'Oh, no— Beth, I'm pregnant. I can't lose it.'

*Please, no…*

'Let's get a look at you,' she murmured.

'Come and lie down here on this other bed and I'll get the ultrasound and we'll have a look, OK? How many weeks are you?'

'Sixteen—no, seventeen. I don't know.'

About what she'd been when she'd found out she was pregnant with Grace, when she'd put her tight clothes down to comfort eating after Ryan had gone away...

'Can I borrow the FAST scanner, please?' she said, and Emma brought it over to her and handed her the gel as Louise pulled her trousers down over her little bump. She could see the mark of the seat belt over her hips. Was the baby high enough to have escaped injury?

*Please let it be all right...*

A nice, steady heartbeat filled the room, and Ryan lifted his head and met her eyes, his expression startled.

'Baby's fine,' she said to Louise, choking back tears, and Ryan's shoulders dropped and he went back to dealing with the boy.

'Are you OK?'

She didn't pretend not to understand.

'Yes, Ry, I'm OK. The baby was fine, Louise is in the antenatal ward under observation, Tim's doing well in PICU, and her husband's trying to split himself in half. I'm happy with that.' She cocked her head on one side and searched his eyes. 'What about you?' she asked softly.

He shrugged and turned away, busying himself with his fancy coffee machine. 'Just another day at the office,' he said lightly, reaching for a mug, but she shook her head.

'No, it wasn't. What did you mean by "I didn't want to lose this one"?'

He shrugged again, but she wasn't having it and she turned him gently to face her. 'Ry, talk to me.'

He let his breath out on a huff, put the mug down and folded his arms across his chest.

'He was called Raoul. He was six, and he used to hang around the medical centre hoping for food. One day he got caught in an explosion, and a small lump of concrete hit him in the chest. I didn't get to see him in time, and by then it was too late. There was too much blood under the pericardium and his heart gave up and I couldn't get it going again. And then I had to tell his mother. It's a sound you never get used to, the wail of a mother who's lost their child—'

He tilted his head back, but she could see

the tears he refused to shed, and she wrapped her arms around him and held him close.

'I'm sorry.'

His arms went round her, his head resting against hers, and they stood like that for a long time.

'There were too many children like Raoul,' he said eventually. 'Babies, little kids, all caught in the fallout, and then the teenagers, the ones who'd joined a militia movement and got themselves shot. Kids who died of diseases we can cure so easily. Malaria, bilharzia, and things like Ebola which are much harder and wipe out whole families. It's just endlessly heartbreaking.'

'Is that why you came home?'

He nodded slowly. 'I had burnout, I think, or if I didn't, I was getting dangerously close to it. That's why I wanted to be here, why I wanted the job, not another one in an inner city fighting to stem the tide of gang violence and drug culture. I just wanted to be normal, Beth. I wanted to feel safe. Is that so wrong?'

'No. No, it's not wrong, Ryan. It's human— and you're still a great doctor, and you're needed here. Without you and the rest of the team, little Tim could have died today, but he didn't, because you spotted it, even though it wasn't that obvious at first.'

'No. He's got Raoul to thank for that, so maybe his death wasn't in vain.' He dropped his arms and stepped away, letting his breath out on a long, slow sigh, then he met her eyes and smiled gently. 'Are you sure you're OK?'

She nodded. 'Yes. Yes, I'm fine. Fancy something to eat?'

'That would be good. I'll take Tatty out while you sort it. And then an early night, I think.' His eyes were warm and tender, and she smiled up at him, and went up on tiptoe and kissed his cheek.

'Sounds perfect,' she said softly.

It was the following Monday and she was walking the dog when her phone rang. Ryan.

'Where are you?' he said brusquely.

'By the river, with Tatty. Why? Where are you?'

'On my way home. I'll come and join you.'

'OK. We'll wait for you outside the pub. Can you bring the car? Tatty's a bit tired.'

'OK. See you shortly.'

The phone went dead, and she stared at it, puzzled. He'd sounded—weird? Very short, which wasn't like him.

'Are you OK, Tatty? Let's go and sit down and wait for Ry, shall we?'

She wagged her tail, but she'd lost the spring in her step and Beth wondered how soon she'd go into labour. If they only knew exactly when the pups were due.

They walked slowly back to the Harbour Inn and found a table outside the front, and Tatty lay down with a sigh at her feet while Beth kept an eye out for his car, her nerves on edge.

What was going on? Had the other guy got the job? Please, no. Not that. Anything but that, but it had been a week now since his interview, two weeks since Ryan's, although they'd been trying not to think about it. Surely they'd decided by now?

His car turned into the car park, and he slotted it into a space, slammed the door and strode over to her, his face tense.

Oh, no. She stood up and took a step towards him, and he stopped.

'I've got a second interview this Thursday,' he said, his voice strangely tight. 'We both have.'

'Why?'

He shrugged. 'They couldn't decide. The panel were divided, apparently. James couldn't say a lot, but he was obviously on my side from the few things he did say. I don't know. I hoped it would be over, but it goes on.'

She hugged him, and he hugged her back, his head resting against hers as he sighed.

'I hate interviews,' he mumbled. 'The last one was vile, and this one—well. Who knows? I can only do my best, and I'm sure there'll be other jobs. Just not here. Ah, well. Fancy eating here?'

'Not really,' she said quietly, feeling crushed for him and gutted that he still didn't know, that they still didn't know, when she'd finally realised how very important it was to him to stay here in this place that meant so much to them. 'Tatty's quite tired. Let's just go home.'

Or home for now, at least.

*Please let him get the job...*

If he'd thought the first interview was gruelling, the second was much worse, the questions designed to challenge even the strongest candidate, but he knew what they were doing. Piling on the stress to see how he coped.

Well, he could do stress. He'd lived on a knife edge for over two years and kept his head, and he kept it now, making sure he addressed his answers not only to the person who'd asked the question but to the others as well, and when it was over he went back to work, resigned to another week or so of torment.

And then the following afternoon James came and found him and put him out of his misery.

She heard the scrunch of tyres while she was in the kitchen, and she met him in the hall. He was early—and he was never early. Why?

'I got it,' he said, looking slightly shocked. 'I got the job. I actually got the job!'

'Oh, Ry!' Her eyes welled, and she threw herself at him and he picked her up and swung her round, his laugh echoing in her ears, and then put her down, cradled her face and kissed her senseless.

She could feel his smile against her mouth, and she pulled away and looked up at him, searching his eyes and finding nothing but relief.

'How did you find out?'

'James told me. He said the panel were still divided, but much less so. Apparently I interviewed really well yesterday and I was much more convincing, but it's gone on so long now I'd begun to think I didn't stand a chance.'

She frowned. 'Why? The other candidate is much older than you, and I thought James felt he was ready to wind down.'

'He did. He still does, but some of the others felt he was a safer pair of hands, and it's my first consultancy and I haven't exactly had a conventional career path in the last few years.'

'So what swayed it in the end?'

He shrugged. 'My interview yesterday, I think. The CEO had the casting vote, so it was his decision.' He laughed. 'Looking at it cynically from his point of view, I'm cheaper, and I'm already here, so they don't have to wait six months for him to work his notice. That's got to help. And James was pretty adamant, I think, from what he said—plus he seems to have realised something's going on with us and I don't think he wanted to lose you, too.'

She narrowed her eyes. 'Have you said anything to him?'

His mouth twitched. 'I might have let something slip.'

'You are so naughty.'

'Yeah, but you love me,' he said.

There was a breathless silence, and then she smiled.

'Yes, I do,' she said softly, and went up on tiptoe and kissed him again. Just a fleeting kiss, and then she sank back on her heels and looked into his eyes.

They were suddenly bright, and he swallowed hard, his hand coming up to cradle her cheek.

'It's been so hard waiting, not knowing what was going to happen, but now...'

'Now we have a future here?' she suggested, holding her breath, and he shrugged.

'I hope so—or at least a shot at it. That's up to you. If it's what you want—'

'Of course it's what I want!'

'Good. I'd better ring James, then, and tell him I'll take it.'

She felt her jaw drop. 'You haven't told him?'

'No. Not till I'd spoken to you.'

'Why?'

His shoulders lifted in a tiny shrug. 'I didn't do things right with Katie. I told her I was signing up with MFA, I told her what it meant to me, that I'd be away maybe for years, that I didn't want kids any time soon if at all—I thought she understood, but I never asked her what she wanted, I just assumed she'd be fine with it, but it turned out she wasn't, and so she tried to manipulate me by getting pregnant. And yes, she didn't handle it well, but nor did I and we both got hurt. I don't want to make the same mistake again.'

'I'm not Katie, Ryan, and you're not the man you were then. Phone James, tell him you want the job, if you really do, but don't do it for me. Do it for yourself. This has to be right for you, and if it's not what you want, then don't take it. I don't want you turning round to me in six months' or three years' time and accusing me of making you do something you didn't want to do.'

He kissed her gently. 'You're not. And I do want it.'

'So ring him. Ring him now, and while you're doing that I'll finish getting supper. Oh, and is your DJ OK? You've got to wear it tomorrow for the wedding.'

'It's fine, it's all ready. I'll ring James now.'

He kissed her again, then pulled out his phone and she went back to the kitchen and stared out of the window at the river in the distance.

It was happening. He was staying, and maybe he'd buy this house and they'd live here together, with that beautiful view in front of them.

With a family?

Her heart thumped. Too soon to think about that. She wasn't ready, and just to be certain, she'd gone back on the Pill. Not that it had worked for them last time, but that was because she'd failed to take it on time in the hectic week leading up to their weekend. She'd be more careful this time, and in the meantime Ryan was being meticulous.

But—maybe one day?

Or maybe not. She frowned. He still hadn't said he loved her. She'd given him the perfect chance, and he hadn't taken it. Why not? And now she knew he'd want children in the future, maybe he was holding back until he was sure she was ready for that. And she wasn't sure she was, or would ever be. It was only two years ago that she'd lost Grace. It seemed like yesterday, but in another lifetime.

Was she ever going to be brave enough to try again?

'All done. He said he'll see us tomorrow at the wedding. So, my clothes are sorted. What are you wearing?'

She pasted on a smile and turned to face

him. 'I don't know yet. I'm sure I've got something. I'll have a look tomorrow.'

'You're on duty from seven to five. You changed your shift, remember, so you didn't have to work on Sunday?'

She clapped a hand over her mouth. 'I'd forgotten. I'd better have a look tonight, and I might as well stay at home if I'm at work for seven. Is that OK?'

'Of course it's OK. We're not joined at the hip, Beth. You can do whatever you like.'

Did she imagine it, or did that sound like he didn't care?

No. He might not have said he loved her, but she knew he cared about her. Just maybe not enough…

'What?'

'Hmm?'

'You've got a strange look on your face, as if I just said something weird.'

'No. Just—"do what you like" sounded a bit…'

'Like I don't own you?' He laughed softly and pulled her into his arms, staring down into her eyes with a smile. 'I simply meant you don't need my permission to do something. It would be nice if you let me know you aren't going to be around just so I'm not worried about you, but you can do whatever you want, of course you can.'

'Are you sure? Because really, I could do with spending this evening at home. I've got so much to do, I haven't done my washing for days and—I don't know, Tatty's beginning to look a bit imminent and if I need to be here I could do with sorting out some clothes and also working out what I'm wearing tomorrow. Would you mind if I go as soon as we eat?'

'Of course I don't mind.'

'Are you sure? Because we probably should be celebrating your new job, and I'm going to take myself off.'

He laughed and hugged her. 'Of course I don't mind. I've got to write a formal letter of acceptance, anyway, and I could do with settling Tatty in whatever place she wants to have her pups. Any ideas?'

'She keeps hanging out in the spare room, at the end of the wardrobe. There's a space there, a bit tucked away? I've found her there a couple of times in the last few days.'

'Yes, so've I. OK. I'll make her a bed. So, what are you cooking? It smells good. Anything I can do to help?'

She smiled up at him, kissed his cheek and handed him the vegetable knife.

It felt odd being back in her own house for the first time in days. Odd, and a bit lonely, but she had plenty to do, starting with putting on a load of washing and then finding a dress for the wedding.

Easier said than done, but it was too late now to worry about it, and she had a few options, one of which was a dress she'd worn the only other time she'd been to the hotel. She'd been going to wear it for dinner, but she'd put it on and they hadn't made it through the door.

She pulled it out and looked at it critically. It was certainly smart enough, a midnight blue velvet dress with a scoop neck front and back, gently figure-hugging with a straight cut and a subtle slit up the back to just below the knee. Discreet, simple, elegant—and he'd taken one look at her in it, peeled it off her and made love to her slowly and systematically, kissing every inch of her and taking her to the brink over and over again until she'd been begging him to finish it.

Would he remember?

She wriggled into it—a little tighter than

it had been, but then she'd been reeling from Rick's lying, cheating betrayal and she hadn't been eating a lot. But it still fitted, better now if anything, and it was the best thing in her wardrobe.

She found earrings and a necklace that were perfect with it, nude heels that weren't so high she couldn't dance in them, and a nude wrap in case it got chilly if they went out into the courtyard, because it was only early May.

She closed her eyes briefly, then put the dress on its hanger and went downstairs, picking up the little heart. This time two years ago, their baby had still been alive. They'd been lonely and heartbreaking years, but now there might be light at the end of that long, dark tunnel.

'Your daddy got the job, my darling,' she told Grace softly. 'He's going to be here, and maybe we're going to be with him, if it all goes well.' She smiled sadly. 'I think you'd like him. I'm so sorry you'll never get to meet him, but I think he loves you. We'll be thinking about you tomorrow, my love.'

She kissed the little heart, then carried it upstairs and packed it in the bag of things she'd got ready to take to Ryan's. She was going to drop it off on her way to work in the morning then come back here after her shift to get ready, and he was picking her up in a taxi at twenty past seven.

And she was already getting nervous, wondering if she was reading too much into their relationship, hoping she wasn't investing too much of herself in him.

Her phone rang, and it was Ryan.

'You OK?'

'Yes—I've got a dress, so I'm all good. How's Tatty?'

'She seems to like that corner. I found a cardboard box in the garage left over from the pictures, so I've cut it down and put a blanket in there for her, and she seems perfectly happy. I think she's getting close.'

'I think so. Are you OK? Coming down off cloud nine?'

He chuckled. 'Yes, I'm fine. Tired. I think the suspense got to me. I might have an early night. You take care, and I'll see you tomorrow evening.'

'You, too. Let me know if anything changes with Tatty.'

'I will. Sleep tight. It'll be odd without you.'

'It's only one night. I'll be with you tomorrow.'

'Good. I'm looking forward to it.'

He hung up, and she put the phone down, the words 'I love you' still hovering on her lips, but he'd gone before she'd had a chance to say them. Just as well, maybe.

# CHAPTER NINE

HE WAS WALKING down her path looking drop-dead gorgeous in his DJ when she opened the door, and he stopped in his tracks.

'Is that the dress…?'

The butterflies were having a field day inside her, and the look in his eyes did nothing to settle them down.

'I wasn't sure if you'd remember it.'

He laughed, a slightly strangled sound, and ran his finger round his collar. 'Yeah, I remember it. Even though you only had it on for—oh, maybe thirty seconds?'

And then he smiled, a tender smile full of promise. 'I might let you wear it a little longer tonight, so I can enjoy it. You look beautiful, Beth. Absolutely beautiful.'

He took her hand and met her eyes. 'Are you OK?' he asked, his eyes sober now, and she nodded.

'Yes. I am now. It's been a bit of a funny day.'

'I'm sure.' They were silent for a moment, Grace in both their thoughts, and then he sucked in a breath and straightened up, holding out his arm. 'Shall we go?'

He held the taxi door for her, then went round and got in the other side. 'So,' he said, turning to face her and deftly changing the subject, 'who's going to be there that I might know?'

'Oh, Ed and Annie, definitely. Ed and Matt were at school together. And James and Connie, and Sam and Kate, Jenny, my line manager, and her husband. I think he's called Peter. Matt and Livvy, obviously. You've worked with both of them. Otherwise I have no idea. I only know her from work and I think they've got lots of friends and family, but it should be a lovely wedding. He's got two little children, a girl and a boy, and his wife died of a brain haemorrhage when they were tiny. That was the same year as Grace, so not long ago. And Livvy's had breast cancer, so it's been pretty emotional for them all.'

'Wow. I had no idea. They never give the impression of being sad.'

She gave a tiny huff of laughter. 'Do we?'

He reached out and took her hand, squeezing it gently. 'I guess not. Are you really OK?'

She smiled at him, not willing to lie and yet wanting to enjoy this evening with him.

'Yes, Ryan. I'm OK. Grace isn't far from my thoughts, but then she never is, and I want to enjoy tonight. Can we do that?'

'I'm sure we can,' he murmured.

The taxi pulled up outside the hotel, and he asked the driver if he could do the return trip. 'What time is it winding up, Beth?'

'I don't know, but I don't want to be late. Can we leave at half ten?'

'That's fine. I don't want to be late, either. Tatty was a bit restless.'

He spoke to the taxi driver again, paid him, and then offered her his arm as they walked towards the hotel, the place where it had all begun.

Strangely fitting, and yet oddly she hardly remembered anything about it once they were inside. They'd either been in their room, or in the dining room, or out and about in the town, strolling by the sea, walking by the river, listening to the sound of the surf and the keening of the gulls, and as far as the hotel was concerned, they could have been anywhere.

They were ushered into a large and beautiful function room, and Matt and Livvy were standing there greeting their guests, looking ridiculously happy and utterly in love.

'Congratulations, Livvy,' she said softly, giving her a gentle hug. 'I'm so happy for you both.'

'Thank you. And thank you for coming. It's so lovely to have you here, and I'm really glad you brought Ryan. I hope things work for you.'

She smiled at the innocent remark, because like everyone else, Livvy only knew that they'd once worked together and that they were seeing each other now. Nothing more, but that was fine. She wasn't sure she knew much more than that herself.

'Thank you,' she said, and hugged Livvy again before turning to Matt and hugging him, too.

And then Ryan was at her side again, his hand resting on her waist as they looked around.

'Matt says there's a bar over there, so shall we?'

She pasted on a bright smile. 'I think that

would be a great idea. Maybe we can find something fizzy to celebrate your job.'

'Good plan.'

Her dress was going to kill him.

There was live music playing quietly in the background, and the hubbub of voices from the colourful throng, but his eyes kept being drawn back to Beth. She was radiantly beautiful tonight, and yet when he looked deep in her eyes there was that lingering sorrow that never quite left them.

They mixed and mingled, chatting to the people he'd worked with over the past five weeks, people who might become friends, and they seemed genuinely delighted that he'd joined the department. They were a similar age to him and Beth, a little older but not much, and he could see why James might have been wary of an older consultant coming in.

'I'm so glad it's you,' his new clinical lead said to him in a slightly indiscreet moment. 'That stuffed shirt would have driven me insane.'

Ryan laughed. 'Yeah, me, too. Just a few minutes in his company was enough.'

'Tell me about it. I'm absolutely sure he's

a great doctor, mind, but he's so pompous. It never would have worked. You, on the other hand—I can mould you.'

Ryan laughed. 'You can try. Many people have. But to be fair, I think we work in a very similar way.'

'Nah. You're more like Sam. He's a bit of a wild one. Ex-army. Bit like you, seen it, done it, knows how to fix it. He may not be entirely orthodox, but he saves lives and that's what it's about.'

'Maybe you needed your box ticker.'

'No, thank you. You're fine. Have another drink.'


'What was that about?'

Ryan smiled at her a little wickedly. 'Oh, just our clinical lead being a little indiscreet.' He looked across the room, then back to her. 'I think the dancing might be about to start. I can see Matt and Livvy over there by the band. Want to go and watch?'

'Oh, I do. She's been making him practise, apparently.'

Their dance was beautiful, the song outrageously romantic, and once it was over the guests headed onto the dance floor to join them.

The tempo picked up at that point, the music morphing into the classic cheesy wedding songs that everyone knew, and Ryan turned to her, held out his hand and smiled. 'Dance with me?'

'Sure. Why not?'

She took his hand and let him lead her into the throng, wondering what kind of a dancer he would be.

Good, was the answer, and he seemed to enjoy it, which was great news as she loved dancing, so she relaxed and threw herself into it, and he shot her a grin, twirled her into his arms and they had a ball.

'Oh, I can't, I need to stop, I've got a stitch,' she said, breathing hard and clutching her side, and he chuckled and led her off the dance floor.

They went to the bar and got some fizzy water, and she rolled the ice-cold glass against her face and sighed.

'Oh, that's good. I haven't danced like that for years.'

'No, nor me. Out of practice.'

'You didn't look out of practice.'

Their eyes locked, and then the music slowed and he put down his glass and held out his hand.

'Dance with me again,' he said softly, and she let him lead her to the dance floor, turned into his arms and settled against him as if they were made for each other. She could feel his hands resting lightly in the small of her back, and she slid her arms around his waist and rested her head on his shoulder.

It felt so good. So right. If only she was sure he loved her...

She shut off that train of thought, and as they swayed together to the music she closed her eyes, stopped thinking and let herself feel.

'It's nearly ten thirty,' he murmured, and she lifted her head, dragged back to reality.

'We need to go. The taxi will be here.'

'Matt and Livvy are over there. Let's go and say goodbye.'

Two minutes later they were standing outside waiting for their taxi, and she shivered.

'I forgot my wrap.'

'Here, borrow my jacket,' he murmured, shrugging it off and draping it round her shoulders.

'So chivalrous.'

'Of course. Not to mention warm. It got quite hot in there.'

It had, in all sorts of ways, but she was cold now, counting down the time.

The taxi pulled up at his house, and they went in and the first thing he did was check Tatty.

She was in her box, and she lifted her head and licked his hand, then got awkwardly to her feet and headed for the door.

'I'll just take her outside.'

'Is she all right?'

'I think so.'

He went with her into the garden, and she wandered round a little, then bopped down for a wee and came back to him, tail waving gently, and pressed her head against his leg.

'Are you OK, little lady?' he asked her softly, but she just headed back inside to her box, and he went to look for Beth.

He found her in his bedroom, sitting on the bed holding the little silver heart in her hands, and when she looked up there were tears on her face.

He crouched down in front of her and rested his hands over hers.

'Are you OK? Would you rather be alone?'

She shook her head. 'No. Sit with me.'

So he sat beside her, his arm around her shoulders, and remembered Grace.

It could have been yesterday, it was so clear.

He was on duty that night and still at the hospital when she rang him.

'It feels weird. Something's different. I'm coming in,' she'd said, and he met her in Maternity reception.

They were taken to a side room, and she was put on a monitor and they watched as Grace's heart slowed, the beats fading to nothing.

He'd never forget Beth's anguished cry, or the howl of pain inside him that had been so unexpected. He'd heard that cry so many times during his aid work, the wail of a parent when a child died.

'Ry?'

He felt her fingers on his cheek now, wiping away tears he hadn't known he'd shed, and he blinked them away and met her eyes.

They were dry now, as if the moment had passed and she was at peace, and she lifted the little heart to her lips, then gave it to him.

'We need to put her somewhere safe,' she said, and he nodded and got to his feet, his daughter's ashes cradled carefully in his hand.

'How about the study?'

She nodded, and he went in there and placed the little heart on his desk, then kissed his finger and touched it to the cool metal. 'Sleep tight, my precious girl,' he murmured, and then went back to Beth.

She was standing waiting for him by the bed, and she cradled his face and wiped away his tears.

'Make love to me, Ry.'

He let his breath out on a huff. 'Are you sure?'

She nodded. 'Yes. Yes, I'm sure. I need you.'

He stared down at her for the longest time, his eyes searching, then gently lowered his head and took her mouth in the sweetest, tenderest kiss.

She felt the moment it changed. It was still tender, and there was no urgency, but she felt the passion welling in him, the need to be close. He stepped away, stripped off his clothes and came back to her, then with a wry and gentle smile he took hold of the hem of her dress and peeled it off over her head, closing the gap between them with a groan.

Still holding her, he led her to the bed and

threw back the covers. She lay down and held out her arms to him, and he followed her down, gathering her up against his chest, his mouth finding hers again.

He took his time, his touch gentle and sure, and when it was over he cradled her in his arms as she drifted off to sleep.

He heard a sound.

Nothing much, just a tiny whimper, and he eased his arm out from under Beth's head and went out into the hall.

A definite whimper, from Tatty. He went into the other bedroom and found her circling restlessly in her bed, and he went back into his bedroom.

'Beth? Beth, wake up. I think Tatty's in labour. Mind your eyes, I need to put the light on.'

She propped herself up on one elbow, blinking slightly, and he pulled on clean clothes and went back to the dog, kneeling down beside her.

'Are you OK, sweetheart?' he asked softly, and she pressed her head into his hand and gave a little groan.

Definitely in labour. He dredged up a memory from his youth, of sitting on the kitchen floor in the semi-darkness, watching his father's black lab giving birth to a litter of eight fat little puppies.

Please God not eight. Two or three, maybe four, even, but not eight. And, more importantly, please let them be all right. He couldn't bear it if they weren't, not today, of all days.

Beth came quietly into the room and stood behind him.

'How is she?'

'Uncomfortable, I think. No puppies yet, but she's working on it.'

'Cup of tea?'

He smiled up at her in the dim light. 'That would be amazing.'

He shifted so that he was sitting near her box, leaning against the bed so he could watch her without crowding her, and Beth brought the tea in and sat down beside him.

'I know nothing about this,' she murmured. 'Well, not from a dog perspective.'

'I don't suppose it's a lot different,' he said, hoping the outcome would be, at least, and his heart squeezed. 'Hopefully she'll know what's going on and will instinctively do the right thing, but I don't think we should leave her. The vet didn't think she'd ever had a litter, she's too young and her nipples didn't look as if she'd lactated.'

'Reg would have known if she'd had puppies and he would have mentioned it,' Beth said, and then added thoughtfully, 'I wonder what they'll look like? We have no idea who the father is. They could be a bit weird.'

He chuckled quietly. 'They could. Let's just hope he wasn't huge. A couple of nice little puppies would be perfect.'

'I think you'll get what you're given, Ry. I'd settle for them all being OK,' she said philosophically, and sipped her tea, then rested her head on his shoulder with a quiet sigh.

He turned his head and pressed his lips to her hair, wondering what was going through her mind. Probably the same as his—

Tatty moved, stretching out her back legs with a tiny grunt, then turning and licking herself, and he peered at her.

'Are you OK, Tatty?' he murmured softly, but she ignored him, concentrating on whatever she was doing.

Licking a puppy?

He leant forwards, and saw two black paws and a black nose, then with another grunt the puppy slithered out, and she licked it furiously, pushing it almost roughly until they heard a tiny squeak.

'Oh! It's alive!' Beth said, and he could hear the joy in her voice.

'Looks like it. And she seems to know what to do.'

They watched her, spellbound, as she nosed the puppy until it was lying by her teats, then it started to suckle and she lay down again, resting but keeping an eye on it until she became distracted.

'I think there's another one coming,' he murmured.

'Will the first one be all right or will it be in her way?'

'We can move it if we have to. She'll probably be OK.'

Beth turned her head and looked at him. 'Have you seen this before?'

He nodded. 'Once. Our dog had puppies. I was probably about seven or eight? That's when I decided I wanted to be a vet.'

'A vet? Am I missing something?' she asked softly, her voice slightly incredulous.

He gave a low chuckle and shook his head, then his smile faded. 'No. I changed my mind when my father was dying. I was twelve when he was diagnosed with cancer, fifteen when he died. I wanted to be able to do something, and of course I couldn't, but I spent a lot of time visiting him in hospital off and on, and it sort of rubbed off on me. Here we go,' he added, leaning forwards again to watch closely, but this time there was a problem.

'It's breech,' he said tightly. 'All tail and bottom, no feet. She might struggle. I'll give her a moment, then I might have to help.'

'How?'

'Gentle traction. If that doesn't work, then the vet.'

Nothing happened, and Tatty was clearly struggling, so he shook his head, picked up a towel he'd put ready and gently grasped the puppy's hindquarters and eased it down and out with her next contraction.

'There we go,' he said, his fingers clearing the membranes away from its face, but it didn't breathe, despite Tatty licking it furiously, so he picked it up, held it in his hand as he'd seen his father do and swung it down to drain the fluid from its lungs.

Nothing. He did it again, and again, and again, and then finally there was a tiny cough, and he grabbed the towel and rubbed it gently, and it squeaked.

'Oh, Ry,' Beth said, and he swallowed hard and put the squeaking puppy back with its anxious mother. She washed it firmly, tumbling it around by her teats, and then nosed it up to lie beside its sibling.

It latched on after a moment, and he gave a sigh of relief and slumped back against the bed, and Beth tucked her arm through his and hugged it. 'Well done,' she said, her voice choked, and he turned his head and kissed her wordlessly.

No choice. He couldn't have spoken if he'd tried, but the pup was OK, Tatty was OK, and all they could do now was watch and wait.

The next two puppies arrived without event, and then after washing them all again and giving them time to feed, Tatty got carefully to her feet and stepped out of the box, looking at them expectantly.

'I imagine she needs to go out,' Ryan said, and left Beth there with the puppies while he took her in the garden.

She shuffled over to them and looked at them closely. Two black, one a pale cream, the other, the smallest and the one who'd had problems, a darker gold, all fat little butter-balls with Tatty's black nose.

They came back, and she got up and moved out of the way so Ryan could clean out the box and give them fresh bedding.

'Here, cuddle the puppies,' he said, handing them to her, and she sat on the bed and cradled them in her lap while Tatty sniffed them and wagged her tail.

'You're a clever girl,' she said fondly, and looked up at Ryan. 'Four's nice.'

He laughed and looked at her over his shoulder. 'I wonder if we'll still be thinking that when they're tumbling round the kitchen causing havoc,' he said, and spread out fresh newspaper in the bottom of the box.

'There you go, Tatty. In you get.'

He scooped up her babies and put them back in the box, and she stepped carefully over them and lay down again with a quiet sigh, the puppies snuggling up to her in a sleepy heap.

He straightened up with a smile, and held out his hand. 'Come on. Let's go and have some breakfast. I'm starving. I didn't eat a lot last night.'

'No, nor did I. What time is it?'

'Quarter to six.'

She swallowed. Two years ago she'd been lying in a side room in the maternity unit cradling her daughter, her world in pieces, and now, all thanks to Tatty and Ryan, the date had a new, happier memory.

She reached up her hand and took his, and he pulled her to her feet, and as if he understood he put his arm around her and walked with her out to the garden.

'How do you fancy a bacon sandwich?'

'Amazing,' she said, conjuring up a smile, and he kissed her gently.

'Sit here in the sunshine. I'll bring you some coffee while the bacon's cooking.'

She perched on the wall and hugged herself, rubbing her arms. It was a bit chilly, but the sun was just coming over the roof of the bungalow and she could feel the warmth of its rays on her head and shoulders. It wouldn't be long before it was summer, she realised. Just another few weeks. By the time the puppies were ready for rehoming, it would be glorious out here.

'You need a new bench,' she said as he emerged with her coffee.

'I do. I also need to talk to the agent about the house.'

'Are you going to buy it?'

'I don't know. I think I'd like to. I love it here. It's so peaceful, and anyway, it's Tatty's home so I sort of have to,' he added with a grin. 'Why? What do you think?'

'What do I think? I think I thought she was going to the rescue centre.'

He pulled a face. 'Yeah. I've been having second thoughts about that, and I don't think Reg would ever speak to me again. I meant the house, by the way. What do you think about the house?'

'I like it,' she said simply. 'You're right, it's lovely and peaceful here, and it's got a beautiful view. And it's Tatty's home, of course.'

He grunted, handed her the coffee and walked away, leaving her smiling.

'I knew you wouldn't rehome her,' she murmured, and wrapped her hands around the mug, the smile lingering.

The puppies were gorgeous, and they'd grown like weeds.

It wasn't long before they were bumbling around the kitchen where he'd moved them to. He'd rigged up a bedroom for them all in the passage that led to the garage, and every now and then they were let out to play, collapsing soon into a heap back in their bed or just falling asleep on their feet and keeling over where they were, usually underfoot.

He and Beth were sharing their care; she'd more or less moved in, and they'd fixed their shifts so that one or other of them was about most of the time, and of course Reg was almost a permanent fixture, turning up every afternoon just after lunch and sitting with the pups in the garden while they tumbled on the lawn.

And because Tatty had been feeding them until they were fully weaned, he and Beth had the luxury of the enormous bed all to themselves, and they were taking full advantage of it.

Life was good, and once the pups were rehomed in three weeks it would be even better, because they'd be working together again, and he missed that, but for now it worked for them, and it wouldn't be long.

Beth was exhausted.

She wasn't sure why. Yes, the puppies had been full on, but she was used to being busy, and work hadn't been any harder than normal. OK, it was summer and there was a small influx of visitors to the town getting into trouble, but that didn't explain it.

Maybe it was the lack of sleep? They'd certainly been staying up late so Tatty could have a last feed before they put her away for the night with the pups, but even allowing for the fact that without fail they'd make love before they went to sleep, she was still getting a solid six or seven hours.

Whatever, she was too tired to eat, not interested in food, and she found her eyelids drooping in the middle of every afternoon regardless of what she was doing.

It was almost as if she was pregnant—

No. She couldn't be. She was back on the Pill, taking it meticulously on time, and until it had kicked in Ryan had been just as meticulous about birth control, so how?

No. She couldn't be—could she? It was either that or something worse, and there was an easy way to find out. Numb, feeling chilled to the bone despite the lovely day, she shut the puppies away with their mum, got in her car and drove to the nearest supermarket, bought a pregnancy test and drove home, then sat in the bathroom for half an hour summoning up the courage to do the test.

And when she finally did, it was positive.

She felt sick. Sick with fear and dread and horror at what this would mean for them, what it would mean to Ryan, because he'd still not said he wanted children yet, or that he wanted a permanent relationship with her, and he still, despite everything, hadn't told her that he loved her.

Because he didn't?

Maybe living together for the last few weeks had made him realise it wasn't what he wanted? Maybe he regretted taking that step and had only done it out of guilt because of Grace?

*How was she going to tell him?*

She heard his key in the lock, and quickly grabbed the test wand and the box and stuffed them into her washbag in the cupboard as he walked in.

'Sorry, I didn't realise you were in here— are you OK?' he added, tipping his head on one side and searching her face.

'I'm fine. Why wouldn't I be?' she lied, and pushed past him. 'Are you going to take Tatty for a walk?'

'Yes, in a second. I just need—'

He broke off, and she held her breath as he walked out of the bathroom after her, a sheet of printed paper in his hand.

The instructions for the pregnancy test.

He looked up, his eyes shocked, then

looked down at it again, dropping it as if it was red hot.

'You're pregnant,' he said, his voice hollow. It wasn't a question. Her face had probably given her away.

He swore viciously under his breath, then strode into the kitchen, called Tatty, clipped her lead on and went out without a word.

So that was it. His reaction, in a nutshell, reduced to a few choice words.

Well, what had she expected? Delight? No. Of course not, because he obviously wasn't ready, didn't want children yet, and maybe never with her. He certainly hadn't wanted Grace, although her death had hurt him deeply, and it looked like he didn't want this baby, either.

Her hand slid down over her still flat abdomen, and she squeezed her eyes shut to hold back the tears.

*Please be all right. Let my baby be all right. That's all that matters.*

She'd be OK. She'd go back to her own house, and Ryan could make his own arrangements for the puppies. Maybe the foster lady could take them now, they were nearly six weeks old.

*Not your problem.*

She went into his bedroom, found all her things and stuffed them into her bag and a couple of carrier bags she found in the kitchen. Her wash things went in, but there was something else, something much more important.

She went into his study, and there on the desk was Grace's heart, but it was sitting on a sheet of paper with Ryan's writing on it, and as she reached out she saw the word 'Grace'.

She picked it up, her heart pounding, and sat down on the chair as if her strings had been cut.

*My darling Grace,*
*I don't know what to say to you, except to tell you that I love you more than I could ever have thought possible.*

*I've lost so much. Your first tooth, your first word, your first step. Taking you to school, taking you to your first dance, walking you down the aisle. All gone.*

*I've never known what it means to be a father, I never had that chance, and I don't know if I'll ever have the chance to find out because, although I love her deeply, I think your mother is afraid to try again, and so am I.*

*But I want you to know that if we ever find the courage to have another child he or she will be told about you, about how much we both love you, and how very much you're missed, every single day.*

*Sleep tight, my beloved angel.*

*Daddy xxx*

The words swam in front of her eyes, and she put the letter down carefully on the desk under Grace's heart, and stood up, her legs trembling.

She had to find him, and she knew just exactly where he'd be...

He didn't know what to do.

This was his fault. It had to be. He'd thought he'd been so careful, and he couldn't remember a single time when he hadn't used a condom, and he'd *seen* Beth taking her pills, because they were in the bedside table and it was the first thing she did every morning without fail, right under his nose.

And yet regardless of that, she was pregnant, but how?

He'd consciously kept using the condoms. He knew the Pill wasn't always reliable. Belt and braces? Maybe, but he'd felt that was better than an unwanted pregnancy—he knew that would devastate her.

Yet here they were. He'd seen the fear in her eyes, the dread of facing what she'd faced with Grace all over again, and it tore his heart to pieces because it had to have been his fault.

But how? When?

Unless...

The night of the wedding, the anniversary of Grace's death.

Of course. They'd made love then, and it had been so unexpected, so emotional, so moving, that contraception was the last thing on their minds. They'd fallen asleep in each other's arms, and he hadn't left the bed until he'd been woken by Tatty whimpering. And at that point, Beth had only just started taking the Pill again, and it wouldn't have had time to work.

*Idiot!* How could he have been so stupid?

He stared out over the river, Tatty lying by his side, her head on his lap as he absently fondled her ears.

How could he make this right? What possible thing could he do to make it better? Nothing, except go back to her and tell her what he now knew, and apologise with all his heart for putting her in this position.

He heard footsteps behind him on the river path, and he braced himself for a cheerful 'Good evening!', but there was nothing, just silence as the footsteps stopped.

Tatty got to her feet, tail wagging, and he saw shoes appear beside him. Beth's shoes.

'I found your letter.'

*Letter?* Realisation struck, and he closed his eyes.

His letter to Grace. He'd written it the day of the wedding, on Grace's anniversary, and he'd put the silver heart on top of the letter on his desk, meaning to show it to Beth if and when the time was right, but the puppies had intervened, and he'd forgotten it in the chaos. Another thing he'd overlooked. *Idiot.*

The shoes moved, and she sat down beside him, leaning against him, tucking her hand in his arm, her head on his shoulder.

'I'm so sorry, Ry. I have no idea how I got pregnant—'

'I have,' he said gruffly. 'It was the night

of the wedding. I didn't use a condom. I didn't even think about it. All I could think about was you, how you were feeling, how sad you were, and I just wanted to make it better, to hold you, to love you, to take away the pain. Only I haven't, I've made it ten times worse. A hundred times worse. And I'm so, so sorry—'

His voice cracked, and he looked away, staring out across the river at the boats swinging lazily at their moorings.

'You said you love me, in the letter. Why didn't you tell me? I needed to know that, Ryan.'

That took him by surprise and he turned to stare at her. 'Of course I love you, but I didn't think you'd want to know. I didn't want to put you under pressure.'

'Under pressure?'

'Yes. Pressure to return my love.'

'But I do, you know that. I'd already told you I love you.'

'Only jokingly.'

She shook her head, her eyes tender. 'I wasn't joking, Ry. Of course I love you. I've loved you since you kissed me here, by the stile, and I've never stopped. All I've done is learn to love you more.'

He studied her face, searching to see if it was true, and he could read it in her eyes, those beautiful eyes that were so very revealing today. Maybe he'd learn how to read them better if he kept on trying. All he needed was a chance...

His eyes were brighter than she'd ever seen them, and he reached out and cupped her cheek in his hand, his fingers trembling slightly.

'I love you,' he said quietly. 'I love you so much, more than I have words to say, and if you give me the chance, I'll tell you every day of our lives together. Marry me, Beth, and let's be a family. You, me, Grace, Tatty—and the baby, if the fates have finished playing with us.'

Her heart hitched in her chest and she felt her eyes well. 'You said Grace.'

'Of course. She'll always be a part of our family, Beth. She's our first child. That will never change.'

His face swam in front of her eyes, and she bit her lips and nodded wordlessly.

'Thank you. For saying that. And yes. Yes, Ry, I'll marry you, and I'll try really hard not to be too scared, but if I am, and if it all goes wrong, just—be there for me, please, like you were before? Because I can't do this without you—'

His arms came round her, crushing her against his chest. 'Never. You'll never be without me, no matter what, so long as I'm alive. I'll never leave you again, I promise you.' He let her go, bent his head and kissed her, his lips lingering on hers to seal the promise, and then he straightened up and smiled into her eyes.

'Come on. Tatty's getting hungry, and I bet the puppies are, too. Let's go home.'

*Home.*

She smiled back at him and got to her feet, tugging him up.

'That sounds like a wonderful idea,' she said, and with his arm around her shoulders and the dog at their side, they walked back along the river path, pausing for a moment at the stile to share another tender, lingering kiss where it had all begun.

He lifted his head and stared down into her eyes, and smiled. 'I love you,' he said. 'Just so you know.'

She smiled back. 'I think I do know now. And I love you, too. Don't ever forget it.'

'I won't.'

Then he put his arm around her shoulders again, tucked her in against his side and walked her home...

# EPILOGUE

'HERE?'

He watched as Beth settled the baby in Reg's arms and walked over to where he was standing poised with a spade. She frowned thoughtfully at the rose they'd found in a garden centre. It was named Grace, and of course they'd had to have it. Now he was waiting for Beth to say where.

'Right a bit, I think. Reg, what do you think?'

The old man smiled. 'It'll be quite a big rose. Maybe a bit more to the right, and back a bit? That's it, Ryan. Perfect. That'll give it room to grow.'

'Like everything else round here,' Beth said with a smile. 'Look at how big Muddle's got, considering how tiny she was to start with. I can't believe we nearly lost her.'

Ryan grunted and glared at the pup, now a

year old and full of nonsense. 'Muddle, no! Get out of the hole, I don't need help digging it!'

He pushed her out of the way, told her to sit and went back to his digging, while she sat poised, riveted by what he was doing, desperate to join in but waiting for the treat she knew was in his pocket.

Tatty was lying on her back in the sun, playing with a raggy toy, and Ryan lifted his head and glanced back at his family.

His wife, their three-month-old baby boy, and Reg, surrogate grandfather to Raoul, named after the boy he still felt he'd failed, the boy whose face he saw in his dreams, but not as often now.

They'd been married ten months, and since then they'd extended the house, making a beautiful kitchen/dining/living space that opened to the garden but with spectacular views from the front of the river and the stile where he'd kissed her at the start of their journey.

They'd added another bedroom, to allow for their family to grow, and although they'd rehomed three of the puppies, one to Ed and Annie, one to James and Connie, and another to the farmer whose black Lab, his gun dog, had turned out to be the father, they'd kept Muddle, the puppy they'd nearly lost, and of course Tatty, who'd brought them all together.

He gave both the dogs a treat, settled the rose into the hole he'd dug for it, and stood back.

'How's that?'

'Perfect,' Beth and Reg said in unison, and he smiled.

'I thought so, too. Better fill it in, then, before Muddle digs it up again.'

He knelt down, pressed the soil in around the root ball and touched the tiny bud just starting to form with the tip of his earthy finger. 'There you go, Grace,' he murmured softly. 'You can grow now. Happy birthday.'

He straightened up, dusted off his hands and went over to Beth, putting an arm around her and the baby. 'OK?'

She nodded. 'Lovely. Look, Raoul. Daddy's planted a rose for Grace. It's going to be so pretty.'

The baby gave her a gummy smile, and she dropped a kiss on his head.

'Happy?' he murmured.

She looked up at him, her eyes a little bright, and nodded.

'Very. Thank you. For everything.'

'Don't thank me. Just having you and Raoul here with me is all I need, all I'll ever need.'

'And Reg and the dogs.'

He smiled. 'Of course. That goes without saying—Muddle, no! Leave it!'

He dived at the dog, and behind him he heard Beth and Reg laughing, the happy sound filling the garden with joy.

He turned back to them with a rueful grin. 'Well, maybe not the dogs...!'

\* \* \* \* \*

*If you enjoyed this story, check out
these other great reads from
Caroline Anderson*

A Single Dad to Heal Her Heart
One Night, One Unexpected Miracle
Their Own Little Miracle
Bound by their Babies

*All available now!*